WHEN ANGELS CRY

WHEN ANGELS CRY

THE UNBELIEVABLE MR. BROWNSTONE BOOK SIX

MICHAEL ANDERLE

LMBPN Publishing
PMB 196, 2540 South Maryland Pkwy
Las Vegas, NV 89109

First US edition, June 2018
Version 1.03, March 2021

Special Thanks
to Mike Ross
for BBQ Consulting
Jessie Rae's BBQ - Las Vegas, NV

Thanks to our Beta Reader
Natalie Roberts

Thanks to the JIT Readers

Mary Morris
John Ashmore
James Caplan
Kelly O'Donnell
Daniel Weigert
Peter Manis
Tim Bischoff
Paul Westman
Larry Omans
Micky Cocker

If I've missed anyone, please let me know!

Editor
Lynne Stiegler

To Family, Friends and
Those Who Love
to Read.
May We All Enjoy Grace
to Live the Life We Are
Called.

T he Light Elf consul paced in front of his massive oak desk, a tablet computer in hand.

Laena forced her face to remain impassive, although the display of a magical being bending the knee so easily to technology disgusted her.

This is what you've let fear do to you. Pathetic. We won't remain strong by imitating humans.

The consul shook his head and stopped. "Multiple murders. Thefts. Breaking and entering. Soul-fed magic. A massive public assault on the Los Angeles Police Department AET, which put several of their personnel in the hospital."

The Drow folded her hands in her lap and said nothing. She would allow the Light Elf his little rant for the moment.

"If the Anti-Enhanced Threat teams hadn't had magical protection amulets the Drow would have slaughtered them." The consul sucked in a breath and shook his head.

"Then it would have been on every television channel for next three months."

Laena allowed the corners of her mouth to turn up, even if she didn't say what she was thinking.

They should be proud they even survived such an encounter, let alone triumphed. It speaks to some minor skill and ability among those humans. Still, Widowmaker must have underestimated them.

The consul shook the tablet. "Do you understand the implications of this, Your Highness?"

The Light Elf's lack of respect would have earned her wrath in any other circumstance, but slaying a Light Elf consul would lead to war. Even refusing to meet with him and disrespecting the Light Elf presence in the city would lead to violence.

The Drow were not ready for that. At least not yet. The Princess had to be recovered before any other plans were considered. Another strategy was in order.

"From what I understand," Laena began, "the human authorities blame the death on a magical human assassin. It's also my understanding that they don't even have the bodies of the so-called murder victims." She gave him a cold smile. "I'm not saying that a Drow was responsible for any of this, but I *am* noting there's little evidence directly linking a Drow to any of these unfortunate events in this twisted and violent city."

The consul scoffed. "We both know that your pet cleaned up her murders by sending bodies to the World in Between. Our own people have found traces of portal magic. We also have consulate staff who witnessed one of your people changing shape."

"Shape-shifting isn't a crime even by human laws. Maybe she just wanted to fit in?"

The Light Elf shook the tablet at her. "It isn't like the old days. There are enough open human magic users now that blatant disregard for their laws will end in them figuring it out. It's not like they don't know about the World in Between." He narrowed his eyes. "And don't think we've not clearly established the use of portal and rift magic by your Drow."

"Again, not a crime, even by human laws."

"Do you think the humans are so stupid?" the Light Elf yelled. "Even if their laws and society haven't caught up with all magic, their government knows what to look for. The only reason they are still clueless is that the consulate took measures." He shook his head. "What do you think would happen if it became public that an Oriceran assassin was rampaging through a city murdering men with impunity and nearly killing police officers? You risked war, even after you were warned."

Laena's face twitched. Even her patience had limits.

War? We only seek to reclaim what is ours.

The two Drow Royal Guards waiting outside the office exchanged glances.

"She's not yelling," one man observed

The other nodded. "Politics."

"She's still going to be angry when she comes out."

"Widowmaker should be happy she's already dead. The

queen would have spent the next twenty years flaying the skin off her body, otherwise."

Both men shook their heads. Inconveniencing the queen was a minor issue. Inconveniencing the queen and *failing* was a grave dishonor.

The red-faced Light Elf set his tablet on the desk and crossed his arms. "My superiors are gravely concerned about this situation, and they've made it clear that they want me to pass along their displeasure to you, Your Highness."

Laena snorted. "I'm well aware of their displeasure, but as I said, even if I *were* to admit a Drow had been involved in all these unfortunate incidents, what would you have me do? We will not prostrate ourselves before the human authorities. Do not insult me by pretending that the Light Elves or any other of the races here always carefully ask for permission for all activities on Earth."

"*Activities*? Is that what you call a murder spree?"

"Perspective is important in all things, so yes."

The consul rubbed the bridge of his nose and let out a long, weary sigh. "May I offer a suggestion, Your Highness?"

Laena nodded, appreciating that the Light Elf was calming down and remembering his place.

"Why not offer the city a gift? You can present it as the Drow being concerned about some of the recent chaos. That way it will come across as goodwill; a group trying to show their respect upon their arrival in this city."

Laena nodded. "I refuse to admit to anything, and the Drow refuse to admit to anything."

"We're not asking you to. We'd prefer it if none of us ever had to explain who that individual really was. It'd only cause trouble for all of us. The humans aren't always that good about distinguishing one Oriceran from another."

The queen allowed herself a sneer. "Are you worried these primitives will descend upon you with their precious technology?"

The consul narrowed his eyes. "Earth and Oriceran are now too linked to focus on how we used to do things. If we want a lasting peace, we must be mindful of everyone's concerns. You can refuse to like that, but it doesn't change the truth."

"Peace? What do humans know about peace? Their history is nothing but constant warfare for the pettiest and most banal of reasons. Some of their leaders make Rhazdon look like a pacifist."

"Be that as it may, this is the reality all races must now contend with, even the Drow."

Laena stood. "Yes. For now."

The consul glared at the Drow queen. "Don't do something like that in my city again."

She sniffed and headed for the door without answering. *I will do whatever I need to for my people, Light Elf.*

———

Shay opened the door of James' F-350 and stepped onto the sidewalk. The dark clouds threatened rain, but so far had only delivered mist. That was still enough water to threaten her coat and the Black Halo slip dress she'd chosen for the evening. She wasn't going to let herself get soaked on her date with James to a fancy Italian restaurant.

She turned back to him before closing the door. "I'm gonna run down to the alley and take a shortcut. It'll be drier that way."

He gave her a nod. "Okay, I'll catch up after I park."

Shay shut the door and hurried toward the alley. The tall buildings on either side kept the alley clear, and she smiled as she stepped into it.

Several footfalls sounded behind her. She tensed.

The nice woman having a date vanished, and the tomb raider and ex-killer took over. She turned to find three large men standing in the alley with wide grins on their face.

The men radiated menace and arrogance. They were several years younger than her and lacked any obvious gang tattoos or colors. They weren't dressed nicely enough for the typical organized crime enforcer, so they were probably nothing more than good old-fashioned freelance thugs.

One of the men leered at her. "Damn, woman. Take off that coat so we can see the rest of those curves."

"Yeah," another man offered. "You've got a smoking body. Why don't we have a little fun?"

Shay sighed. "Just turn around and walk away, assholes. You don't want trouble."

The first man laughed. "Bitch's got a mouth on her. Bet I could put it to good use."

This was just supposed to be one nice night with my man

before I hit a raid, and these assholes had to go and screw that up.

Shay shook her head. She could take these fools down without even chipping a nail, but she had other immediate and practical concerns stopping her.

She crossed her arms. "Look, normally, I'd beat the shit out of you, but I went to a lot of trouble to dress nicely. If I kick your asses, I might tear my dress or break my heels." She shook a foot. "Four-inch heels. Nice."

"Oh, I'm so fucking scared." The men all trembled. "I like feisty, bitch, but don't push it. Maybe you should get on your knees and make nice before we get pissed."

Shay grinned as a shadow fell over the men. "Like I said, I don't want to risk my outfit." She pointed. "So I'm gonna let *him* take care of it."

The men spun to find a glaring and suited James cracking his knuckles.

"Guess I could use a little exercise before dinner," the bounty hunter rumbled. "And I don't think this suit will rip easily."

Shay gave a little wave. "Sorry, boys. Should have taken my advice and just left."

She continued down the alley, her heels clacking against the asphalt. Their sound mixed with the screams echoing from behind her.

———

James held open Palazzo Ducale's door for Shay, annoyed that the pricks had messed up his night. He had already been tense enough about having to eat at a fancy place again with the woman, and she wasn't willing to go to an upscale steakhouse and split the difference with him.

At least Shay was still smiling as she stepped through the door.

She winked. "You might want to wash the blood off your knuckles, sweetheart."

The maître d' smiled from his podium. "Ah, the unbelievable Mr. Brownstone is here tonight."

James blinked and looked at Shay. "I thought you had reservations under your name."

Shay rolls her eyes. "It's called being famous."

"We're so pleased to have you here tonight, sir." The maître d' smiled. "We have a nice table for you and your date tonight, Mr. Brownstone."

James shrugged. "Sure, great. Uh, where are your bathrooms?"

The other man pointed across the dining room. "Just take a right in the hallway, and I'll seat your date."

About five minutes into their soup Shay glanced at James. His stiff shoulders and frown didn't scream that he was having a good time.

"Problem, James?"

"Why are there so many fucking spoons and forks? Is this just some bullshit thing that silverware makers do?"

Shay laughed. "Oh, that's what's bothering you?"

"Just need a knife, fork, and spoon, right?"

"The key to fine dining is the right tool for the right food. Just think about it like a fight. Sometimes you need to stab a guy close up, sometimes you need to shoot a guy not so close, and sometimes you need to blow someone up with a rocket launcher." Shay tapped a fork. "In this case, just go from out to in with each meal course."

"This shit is so complicated. How the fuck can people make even eating complicated?"

Shay gestured to James' napkin. "And put that in your lap."

He grunted and complied, just in time for their waitress. She smiled and laid down two plates filled with cured sausage, olives, anchovies, artichoke hearts, mushrooms, and five different kinds of cheese.

"Even the cheese is complicated," James grumbled.

"Need anything else?" the waitress inquired.

Shay shook her head. "Not for now. Thanks."

James eyed the food like he'd been handed some plate of Oriceran dried insects.

Shay snickered. "Come on, you can eat cheese and sausage at least."

He grunted. "Still not as good as barbeque."

By the end of the meal, Shay was pleasantly surprised. James hadn't embarrassed himself or her, and she couldn't find a reason to be angry at him. Even though he hadn't gotten his precious barbeque, he'd had some authentic Neapolitan Pizza Margherita without bitching too much. Hell, he'd seemed to like it.

There might be hope for you yet, James.

"Got to hit the can again," he rumbled.

Shay snickered. So much for the classy atmosphere, but she'd still take her man, grunts and all.

James stood and navigated through the dining room. His tense motions suggested he was afraid he'd slam into a waiter or knock over some glasses.

Two young women stepped past James as he passed into the hallway leading to the restrooms.

The hems of those dresses are so high they are fucking shirts.

The women stopped, their gazes lingering on James for a moment before they headed back into the dining room.

Shay's stomach knotted as déjà vu settled over her. The two young women sat back down at their table right behind James and Shay's table.

"I wasn't sure from a distance," one of the women murmured. "But up close he's pretty scrumptious. Not like you have to look at his face when you're having fun."

"He sure fills out his suit well. I'd like to find out if he's as unbelievable in bed as he is every other way."

"Oh, I'm sure he is. I bet he can go all night long and then the next day."

Shay sucked in a breath. Opening her heart to love also meant opening her heart to jealousy. She was still learning how to deal with the emotion in a balanced and reasonable manner—one that didn't involve violence.

This just means I made a good choice.

James returned to the dining room and walked toward Shay, a lightness in his step that wasn't there before.

"Oh, here he comes. Let's talk about something else," one of the women whispered.

The bounty hunter grabbed the back of his seat.

Shay held up a hand. "I'm done, and we already paid. You done, or did you want something else?"

James shrugged. "I'm good."

The tomb raider grabbed her purse from a chair beside her. "Then we should get going. But one thing first."

"What?"

She walked to the young women's table. She leaned over the table and gave them a feral grin. "He's way too much man for either of you. You couldn't possibly handle him." She winked. "I'm still sore, and it's a week later."

With that she flounced out calmly, giving them the finger as she walked away. Gasps filled the room.

Yeah, probably won't be able to come back here for a while.

James followed her, not speaking until they were outside. "What the fuck was that about?"

"Just a little friendly girl talk."

"You're not gonna kill them, are you?"

Shay laughed. "I'm the new improved Shay Carson."

"What does that mean? You kill them slowly instead of fast?"

"I don't have to kill *everyone* who pisses me off. Just some of them."

James grunted. "I don't know if that makes me feel better, but I had a good time. The pizza was good."

Shay patted him on the arm. "We'll make a connoisseur out of you yet—or at least a pizza lover."

"If you say so."

2

Why do the fuckers always run?

Trey charged after the bounty. He had to give the guy credit. The bounty moved damned fast for a guy with a huge gut, but the power of fear wouldn't overcome the anger fueling the pissed-off bounty hunter.

"Don't make me knock your punk ass down, Leonard," Trey shouted. "I'm already not in a good mood since you're running."

The other man hopped onto a fence and vaulted over it in one smooth movement. He glanced behind to verify if Trey was still on his ass.

Enough with this parkour shit, bitch.

The bounty hunter leapt onto the fence and replicated the man's move a few seconds later. "I just got these threads. If you make me tear a hole in them, I'm gonna rip you a new asshole. You hear me, Leonard? This suit wasn't cheap."

The bounty kept up his pace although sweat poured down his face and jumped the next barrier, a low-lying wooden fence. Trey closed on the man and jumped over the fence head-first, tackling the bounty. The top points of the fenceposts only narrowly missed snagging his dark suit.

Leonard collapsed to the sidewalk with a grunt, Trey on top of him. The bounty hunter bent the man's arm back, and the criminal squealed in pain.

"Stop fucking fighting me and you won't get hurt. You're a level-one bounty, Leonard. That means you're worth money to me. Otherwise, I wouldn't be here fucking with you. This ain't personal."

The man slumped to the ground, moaning but not fighting anymore.

Trey shook his head. "Was that so fucking hard?" He cuffed Leonard's hands behind his back and pulled him to a stand before dusting his pants off. "You're lucky, Leonard. Looks like my suit is okay."

The other man glanced behind him. His gaze traveled Trey's body for a moment. "Damn, that *is* a nice suit."

"Of course it is. I don't wear rags on the job. I'm trying to maintain a style here."

"Just saying, I'm surprised you would risk the thing. What do you do if someone shoots you?"

"That shits annoying, and it's already happened." Trey pushed the man toward his F-350. "Anyway, I'm with the Brownstone Agency, bitch. We do whatever it takes to get the bounties, just like the big man himself. Hell, I've seen him go the extra mile myself."

"Wait, Brownstone actually runs the agency?"

Trey opened the back door of F-350 and shoved Leonard in. "What the hell did you think? That I just started some business and called it the Brownstone Agency?"

"I thought it was a franchise thing, you know? Like McDonald's. You pay Brownstone money to use his name."

"Bitch, *please!*" Trey circled around the truck and hopped into the driver's seat. "Franchise? I should pop you just for that. Brownstone doesn't need money. The man's a class-six bounty hunter. He could retire to Cabo San Lucas today if he wanted."

He glanced at Leonard. The anger, suspicion, and fear on the man's face had been replaced by curiosity.

Here we go again. I should print up some pamphlets with questions and answers to speed this shit along.

"What's he like?" Leonard asked. "Brownstone, that is."

Trey started the truck. "Brownstone? You know what he's like. He's a motherfucking badass. He's the king of badasses. The man took down the Harriken not just in LA, but in fucking *Tokyo*. Think about that. He did shit the cops and FBI couldn't do, and there's a hell of a lot more of them than Brownstone."

Leonard nodded eagerly. "I heard Brownstone sleeps with like ten women a night."

"Shut your mouth, bitch. Brownstone's a gentleman. He's no man-whore. Ten women a night? I can't even believe you said that." Trey pulled away from the curb.

Leonard's eyes widened. "Wait. Shit! Brownstone drives an old truck. Is this *the* truck?"

"You *wish* it was Brownstone's truck. This is the sole property of me, Trey Garfield." The bounty hunter shrugged. "Ain't saying I didn't get a little inspiration from the big man. It's a classic. You want to be a winner, then do what winners do."

"I heard he killed a guy who got in a fender bender with him because he loves his truck so much."

Trey scoffed. "Brownstone ain't no thug. He's a professional, and he only goes after you if you've got a bounty or you've threatened someone he cares about. Everyone he's taken down has had it coming. If he was killing people when they got in accidents with him, do you think the cops would let him walk free doing jobs?"

Leonard frowned. "I guess not. But, hey, what about that Marine thing? It's bullshit, right?"

Trey turned a corner. "What do you mean? Bullshit how?"

"I mean, the news made it sound like he lured a bunch of hitmen to Camp Pendleton and the Marines captured them. It's not like Brownstone has the military working for him. He's just some bounty hunter."

Trey answered with a snort. "'Just some bounty hunter?' That's the problem with guys like you."

"What?"

"Brownstone understands something a lot of you bitches don't."

"Huh?"

Trey shook his head as he changed lanes. "Respect. Because he gives respect, people respect him, and that includes most of the 5-0 and the military. Nah, the Marines don't work for him, but they did him a favor." Trey laughed. "We also got a former Marine drill instructor as our main trainer and recruiter now at the Brownstone Agency."

Leonard looked glum. "I wanted to join the Marine Corps, but I took the ASVAB and they said I wasn't smart enough."

Trey chuckled. "People like you must be the reason they have to stick 'front toward enemy' on claymore mines."

Leonard muttered under his breath and anger flashed across his face for a moment before the curiosity and eagerness returned. "Hey, is it true that Brownstone maintains a personal gang?"

"Kind of."

"Kind of?"

"What the fuck do you think I used to do before I worked for the Brownstone Agency?"

Leonard blinked. "Shit, *seriously?*"

Trey grinned "Yeah. Brownstone's turning criminals into criminal *hunters*. We're gonna clean up this town, and little old nanas will be able to walk outside in the shittiest neighborhood without fearing pieces of garbage. I bet you in a few years LA will be the safest city in the country. They should rename this shit Los Brownstone."

"Brownstone's doing all that, even though he's a junkie?"

"Brownstone's a junkie?" Trey snort-laughed. "Bitch, what are you talking about?"

"I thought he took a lot of dust. That's why he's so fearless."

"He's fearless because he's a badass." Trey shook his head. "He likes beer, but the only thing he's addicted to is barbeque."

"Barbeque?"

"Yeah. He loves it so much that one time he took a day

trip all the way to Vegas just to go to someplace called Jessie Rae's."

"Must be a hell of a barbeque place if he's willing to drive there all in one day."

"Don't know. Never been. But if the big man likes it, there's a reason." Trey stopped at a red light. "Plenty of good barbeque in LA, though."

"What's the most badass thing Brownstone has ever done?" Leonard inquired. His eyes were lit up like a kid talking about his favorite movie star.

"Most badass? Other than wiping out the Harriken in the US and Tokyo? That's pretty badass."

Leonard nodded. "Yeah. Just, some of the stuff I've heard on the news is hard to believe. It's hard to know what's just bullshit Brownstone's spreading and what's actually true."

Trey rubbed his chin. "Damn. Too many moments of pure badassery to pick from. He beat down King Pyro because that fucker threatened his family, you know? You see that on the news?"

"The bank robber who could melt metal with his bare hands?"

Trey nodded. "Not only that, Brownstone's taken out necromancers, including a body-jumper in Detroit and this fucker down in Mexico who was so badass the Mexican military tried to bomb him out. I want you to think about that. They sent the fucking military after some bastard's ass, and he survived…until Brownstone showed up. That means Brownstone's basically the equivalent of an army."

Leonard whistled. "Yeah, all that Harriken shit gets the news, but they were normal people, not magic freaks."

"Damn right. You know, before he killed the Harriken in Tokyo, they sent all sorts of crazy-ass killers after him. Not just hitmen, but people with serious powers. Magic shit."

"I didn't know that."

"That's because you're a small-time thief, not a big gangster or anything." Trey snorted.

Leonard shrugged. "Man's got to make a living."

"By robbing little old nanas?"

The criminal looked down and cleared his throat. "Let's talk about Brownstone some more."

Trey chuckled. "Fine. Brownstone's willing to take on anyone, magical or not. Not just people from Earth, you know? He's taken down more than a few elf criminals who have all sorts of spooky-boo magic and other shit from Oriceran."

"What about those killers you mentioned? They Oriceran?"

"Nope, humans, but he took down some Oriceran hitmen when the Harriken had that bounty on him."

Leonard shook his head. "I remember hearing about that. Some of my friends thought about going after him. They said it'd be like the Lotto."

"You're still alive, so you must not have gone after him."

"Seriously? I hid in my apartment until all that shit was over."

Trey barked out a laugh. "Good plan. Hitmen who go after Brownstone end up dead or in jail, magical or not. Just like there was this bitch in Tokyo he fought... Well, she was actually German, but she went to Tokyo after him. She sucked up a bunch of souls and had the strength of like a hundred people, from what I heard. No one had won a fight against her in years until Brownstone."

"Shit, are you talking about Sabine Haas?"

"Yeah, that was her name. I wasn't there. I just heard about it later."

Leonard looked stunned. "Brownstone beat the Collector? I thought she was immortal."

"Might have been, until she met Brownstone." Trey turned at an intersection. "Everyone thinks they can take down the big man, but here's the truth: if Brownstone's coming for you, it's safer just to turn yourself in to the police. Because if you've got the big man's attention, you're in for a world of pain."

"Come on!"

"Just think of him like a personal hurricane who has decided to beat your ass down. You can hide from the hurricane, or go find some place to protect you, but you ain't gonna be taking that hurricane out."

"Garfield," Sergeant Mack called from the front counter. "Bring your boy up."

Trey stood, and Leonard followed without even being yanked. The ride over had involved enough bonding that Trey could probably have removed the handcuffs without trouble.

They made their way to the counter.

The bounty hunter chuckled. "You want some Brownstone trivia, Leonard." Trey pointed to the sergeant. "The cop who's about to process your ass was once the landlord of James Motherfucking Brownstone himself."

Leonard stared at Sergeant Mack. "Shit, seriously?"

The cop shrugged. "He was a good tenant. Paid on time, kept the place clean. Never had any complaints."

The criminal shook his head. "I can't believe you know Brownstone personally. Hey, why did he even go after the Harriken to begin with?"

Sergeant Mack tapped his keyboard for a few seconds before answering. "You don't know? I thought everyone knew."

The cop glanced at Trey, and the other man shrugged. He was surprised himself that Leonard didn't know.

The bounty leaned closer and lowered his voice. "I've heard a lot of shit, and some of it's crazy. I've heard the Harriken killed the secret son he had with some Oriceran princess. I've heard that they blew up his house. Shit, I heard that Brownstone got angry because some Harriken asshole cut him off in traffic."

"They *did* blow up his house, or at least someone did because of a bounty." Sergeant Mack shook his head. "But he went after the local Harriken way before that for a different reason."

Trey snorted. "Bitches got what was coming to them. Fucking cowards."

Leonard looked between the two men. "What? Why? What started it all? It's not like Harriken haven't been in LA for a long time."

"The Harriken killed his dog." Sergeant Mack sighed. "They thought they were intimidating him, but all they did was sign their own death warrants."

"*Killed his dog?* You telling me that guy killed hundreds of guys because they killed his *dog?*"

"At first, anyway," Trey interjected. "After that, it was because those bitches didn't get the message and kept trying to send hitmen and shit after him."

Leonard stood there, utter disbelief on his face. "And the cops let him get away with it?" He turned to the sergeant. "I mean, fuck! You even put out a bounty on the Harriken."

Sergeant Mack scoffed. "The police deal with what is reported to us. It's not like the Harriken were calling us up and asking for police protection, and, yeah, eventually the city *did* get an organizational bounty. The Harriken should have kept their noses clean and gone legit. Maybe they'd still be around, then."

Leonard stared at the sergeant wide-eyed. "Shit. Brownstone could have come after me. What if I had pissed him off?"

Trey and Mack laughed simultaneously.

The bounty frowned. "What?"

"Why do you think he has the Brownstone Agency?" Trey adjusted his tie. "I'm tough, but I get that I'm no James Brownstone. Your level-one bounty ain't enough to get Brownstone out of bed unless you got some serious information for the 5-0." He nodded at Sergeant Mack.

Leonard let out a sigh of relief, apparently forgetting he was still in the process of being booked into jail.

A thoughtful look crossed Sergeant Mack's face. "I've known Brownstone for years. Even though he's really upped his game lately because of the Harriken, it's not like he's not always taken down only high-level bounties. It's just with all that Harriken crap, people are paying a lot more attention."

"Like what?" Leonard inquired. "What's the weirdest thing you remember him taking on?"

"We had some sort of weird Oriceran hippo-alligator monster in the sewers a few years back. He took that out."

"Shit, I remember that. They called it the 'Terror Down Under.'"

All three men shared a laugh.

Sergeant Mack nodded. "Yep. Brownstone didn't care. We waded through literal shit to find that thing and take it down. Saved ten city workers the day he got it. In Japan, he took down some Oriceran monster that was getting into people's heads and making them commit suicide."

Trey grinned. "Not just a badass bounty hunter, but the world's most badass pest-control guy."

"Damn," Leonard whispered. "You think I could join the Brownstone Agency after I get out?"

Trey laughed. "Bitch, you wish."

3

James gave Shay a kiss. "Let me know you're alive every now and again."

The tomb raider opened the truck door and stepped into the LAX loading zone outside the desks for the international airlines. She opened the back door to grab her suitcases before she responded.

"You get in more trouble than I do, you know."

James grunted. "Depends on how you define trouble."

Shay pulled her two large suitcases around behind her, then reached in and grabbed a long thin box with a strap and slung it over your shoulder.

James eyed the long box. "You're just gonna check a sword in?"

"Yep. I've got enough gadgets on this to know if anyone tampers with it, and I've got all sorts of paperwork that shows it's a legitimate historical artifact that shouldn't be tampered with by TSA and that sort of shit." She leaned in and winked. "Why smuggle when you don't have to?"

He grunted. She was smuggling tons of guns and knives already.

"You think you'll need it?"

Shay shrugged. "Don't know. Been running into a lot of magical assholes lately. It doesn't hurt to have a few extra options. Try and not piss off any major criminal organizations while I'm gone."

"No promises."

"Then at least wait until I get back before you take them out."

"Okay, *that* I can do."

Shay smiled one last time and closed the door. She moved toward the airport's sliding glass doors, suitcases behind her and her sword slung in a case over her back.

James put the F-350 into gear. He had a few things to take care of himself.

James didn't know what to expect when he knocked on Zoe's door. His last face-to-face encounter with the beautiful potions witch had been awkward even by her normal standards, but she'd still been helpful in hooking him up with a runes witch to help with Alison's room.

The door swung open to reveal the dark-haired gray-eyed witch, and her bloodshot eyes widened in appreciation. The Professor might drink for entertainment, but Zoe drank to maintain her magical abilities. Even after all their conversations, James still had trouble wrapping his mind around the idea.

She wore a high-slit silver dress that revealed a little more of her thighs and cleavage than James was comfortable with. He averted his eyes.

"Good afternoon, James." Zoe gestured into her plant-filled living room. More a jungle, really. However drunk she was, her words weren't slurred.

James stepped inside. "Were you able to get them made?"

She pointed toward a large box filled with dozens of potions. "Let me be clear: these are for normal humans. They'd be dangerous if you used them. Are all your employees humans?"

"Yep, just regular Angeleno humans." He shrugged. "For now. Just want everyone to have a healing and energy potion, just in case."

"But they aren't going after the kind of bounties you are, correct?"

James nodded. "Sure, but a bullet can kill a man as easily as some spell shit."

Zoe let out a sigh. "Such a dangerous line of work."

"It's a dangerous world. Someone has to do something about that."

"I suppose." Zoe handed the box to Brownstone. "Will you ever find peace, James?"

"I don't know about that, but if assholes would stop doing shit like blowing up my house, it'd be better." He stared at the witch. "Am I your only customer who needs all this shit because of danger?"

Zoe shrugged. "I have more than a few who live colorful lives, but most of my customers are either other witches who need specialty potions for their own magic or bored housewives looking for the most minor magic to spice up their lives." The witch leaned in and inhaled deeply. "Ah. You do seem calmer. Now I understand why." She let out a quick giggle.

James frowned. "What are you talking about?"

"Man is fire. Woman is ice. Or yin and yang—however you want to think of it." Zoe lifted a slender finger. "Balance is important, especially for a fire burning as hot as you."

"What are you talking about?"

"Your woman, James. You're with someone now, aren't you?"

James shrugged slightly. "Yeah, I'm seeing someone. No big deal."

"No big deal? A woman who can tame the fire of James Brownstone is formidable indeed."

"That's one way to describe her."

A broad smile took over Zoe's face. "I'm glad you've found someone." She suddenly furrowed her brow and pointed to the box. "The two lavender potions are for the girl—your new daughter."

"Alison? She doesn't need any healing or energy potions."

"Ah, but she's a young woman. She needs beauty. They will help her skin glow."

James frowned. "She's... How will they affect a magical being?"

"Ah, her skin will glow twice as much."

He glanced down at the bottles. He'd drunk enough potions from Zoe to trust her, but he still had no intention of giving his soon-to-be adopted daughter some strange beauty potion. He'd hold on to them for now.

"How much?" James inquired. "You never quoted me a price when I asked for all the healing potions."

"Potions for *normal* humans are easier to make."

James wondered if she had some clear idea just how different he was.

No way she knows I'm an alien.

"So, they're cheaper?"

Zoe nodded. "I don't need any special ingredients this time. I'll just take cash."

He cleared his throat. "Just money? That's unusual."

"Money makes both the worlds go around, James. But to be clear, cheaper isn't the same thing as cheap."

"Saving someone's life never is."

A curious glint flashed in her eye. "You value these men's lives so much?"

"I'm trying to build a company, and that means proving to my employees I give a shit."

Zoe crossed her arms, which had the side-effect of pushing her breasts up. The annoying thing was, James was certain she wasn't doing it on purpose.

"Interesting," the witch offered. "You're many things, James Brownstone, but predictable isn't one of them."

James shrugged. "Okay, I'll pay as soon as you bill me. Thanks for the help. I'll see you around."

"Indeed you will." She offered him a warm smile.

The bounty hunter headed for the door, box in hand. He had a specialty case for storing potions being delivered to his house later that day, but for now, all he'd have to do was avoid getting in a wreck.

That wasn't so bad. Might as well grab some barbeque before I head home.

Bill glanced down at his daughter's tiny hand in his. His heart pounded, and he hoped the little blonde four-year-old didn't realize how concerned he was. Their fun family trip to Vegas was turning stressful.

"We're almost there, Dina. Stay strong."

He took a deep breath and stopped. The bright lights of downtown Las Vegas surrounded them, pushing back the night. A glance to his side revealed a path leading through several of the buildings. They'd be able to avoid having to walk around the entire block, and at least that would get them back in the general area of their hotel.

Or so he hoped.

Why did I have to forget my phone in the hotel room?

Bill advanced into the darkened path between the buildings, not wide enough to be called an alley, really.

"It smells bad," Dina observed, wrinkling her nose.

The girl was right. The stench of urine filled the alley, and Bill assumed homeless men slept between the buildings at night.

Got to sleep somewhere I guess. Just don't want to have to deal with them.

"I'm sorry, sweetheart. We'll get back to the hotel soon. I promise. Then we can order some nice ice cream as a special treat."

"Yay! I want chocolate."

Bill offered her a smile. "I'm sure they have some chocolate."

A minute later, he realized the path wasn't taking them the direction they needed. Bill looked around with a fake smile plastered on his face. A wider alley led to some bright neon-covered buildings on the far end. That would at least get him near someone he could ask for directions.

"We're just going down there for now, sweetheart. I have to ask people some questions."

Dina looked up at him. "I want ice cream?"

"We'll get some."

Footfalls sounded behind Bill.

Okay, we should just keep...walking.

A dark miasma spread in front of them, choking the rest of the alley in shadow.

What the hell is that? Some weird exhaust?

It's just some stupid bum following us. It has to be. Maybe if I just give him a few dollars, he'll go away and I can get out of this weird-ass alley.

Bill looked behind him, expecting a vagrant. His heart kicked up, and bile rose in a throat.

A figure cloaked in shadows stood in the alley. Glowing red eyes pierced the darkness.

"We're going to play a little game, sweetie," Bill whispered.

"A game?"

Bill grabbed Dina and lifted her toward an air conditioning unit sticking out of the side of the building. "Be Daddy's little angel and climb up that and then into that vent."

"That's not a game, Daddy."

"Just be safe." He had no idea what the hell was going on, but it didn't matter as long as he could keep his daughter safe.

He finished lifting her, and she scampered on top of the unit before crawling into the vent.

Bill advanced toward the figure. "Uh, do you need some money or something?"

The red eyes grew closer. "I need something, yes." The voice came out hollow and ragged.

"Do I need to—"

Pain exploded through Bill's chest, and he screamed. He fell to his knees and looked down. A barbed tentacle had impaled him. Every beat of his heart sent another jolt of agony through his body and his lifeblood spilling to the ground.

"I need something," the voice repeated. "I need your life."

Bill barely registered the movement in the shadows before the killer separated his head from his body.

Dina's eyes widened, and tears burst from her eyes. In the shadows of the alley, she couldn't clearly make out what had happened, but she'd seen her father drop his knees and heard him scream. Blood splattered in the darkness, and her father's head fell into the darkness.

Red Eyes advanced toward her.

"You leave my daddy alone!" Dina sobbed.

"Leave him alone? Oh, don't worry. I'm not a monster. I'm not going to eat him. I only needed to kill him."

"You killed my daddy? I'm gonna get you for killing my daddy!" She continued sobbing.

"Yes." Red Eyes inhaled deeply. "Oh, why don't you come down there and play with me, little girl?"

Dina found a small rock in the vent and threw at Red Eyes. He didn't react.

"Don't you want to join your father, little angel?" A taunting chuckle followed. "That's what he called you, didn't he?"

The girl continued sobbing. "I'm gonna go get someone, and they'll punish you. They'll make you go to jail."

The chuckle became a bellowing laugh. "Who in the world is going to come after me? I am Death, and I can kill whatever pathetic person comes for me. Las Vegas is now my territory, and all who oppose me will witness my skill in killing."

His red eyes receded into the darkness along with his laughter. "And, little one, no one is going to come get you! I win either way."

Light returned from the other end of the alley, but Dina was too far to make out anyone or anything. She closed her eyes so she didn't have to see the disgusting scene. Climbing down was suicide with a monster still around.

She took the only option left her. The girl sobbed at the top of her lungs until exhaustion finally took her.

Something rattled in the darkness.

Dina blinked her eyes open. The tall buildings kept the

alley covered in the shadow, but the sun had risen, pushing away the deeper darkness.

The rattle sounded again. The girl crawled from the vent and poked her head into the alley. A dark-skinned middle-aged homeless woman was digging in a trash can on the other end of the alley, pulling out cans and shoving them in a trash bag.

"Help!" Dina shouted. "Help!" She waved.

The woman's head shot up, and she ran toward the girl.

"Little girl, how did you get up here?"

Dina sniffled and crawled onto the air conditioning. "My daddy put me up here to keep me safe from Red Eyes."

"Red Eyes?" The woman's face scrunched in confusion. "And where's your daddy?"

The girl couldn't bear to glance farther down the alley. She closed her eyes and pointed. In the daylight, the splatter of darkened blood was obvious even at a distance. Flies already buzzed above the body and the head.

"Get thee behind me, Devil," the other woman exclaimed. She took several deep breaths and turned away from the carnage.

The homeless woman reached up. "We need to get you out of here."

Dina reached down and took the offered arms. The woman lowered her to the ground and took her hand. She led the girl away from the body toward the front of the alley. After a good thirty seconds of walking, they arrived at a side street.

The homeless woman pulled out a phone. "You just wait here a second, honey. I don't want to be involved in whatever this was, but I'll get the police here for you."

Dina looked the woman up and down. Her ratty jeans and T-shirt, along with her smell and torn jacket, left little doubt about her homelessness in the girl's mind.

"Do you live in a garbage can like Oscar the Grouch?"

The woman chuckled. "No, sweetie. I just live on the street."

"Why do you have a phone then?"

"Because I understand priorities, sweetie." The woman dialed a number and waited. "Yeah, I need to report a murder, and there's a little girl here, too. She was hiding. Yeah, yeah. I don't know. I think it's her dad. Where are we? In an alley." She rattled off an address. "Okay, I'll stay here until you arrive." She slipped the phone into her pocket.

"Who was that?"

"The police. They're on their way, but I've got to get out of sight. I'll be nearby, but I can't get involved with the cops."

Dina bit her lip. "What if Red Eyes comes back?"

"No demon is coming back in daylight. The monsters come out at night. Everybody knows that. Now you just stay right here until the police come, okay?"

The girl nodded. She kept her eyes forward, desperate not to look at her father's body.

The woman rushed down the alley across the street. She stopped at the next street and waved before turning the corner.

Dina stood there for a moment, shaking and not sure what to do. Sirens screamed in the distance, growing closer with each second. The girl sat against the wall and waited for the police to arrive.

A couple of minutes later, two police cars screeched to a halt in front of the alley. Police hurried out of each car and toward the girl.

She burst into tears again at the sight of the police, the shock of the whole experience blasting into her again.

I'm gonna get someone, Red Eyes. Just you wait. I'm gonna get someone to get you for my dad.

4

James pushed the vacuum through his living room. Keeping his new place clean was easy. Hardly a chore, really, if only because it was so empty.

He'd replaced a lot of his furniture, but the real heart of his home, treasures such as his signed recipe books, had gone up in the fire the rocket launcher had caused. A few books formed the start of his new collection, but it'd take years to gather the rest—and some of his books had been irreplaceable.

The bounty hunter grunted as he pushed and pulled the vacuum over the carpet. He needed something to do. Without a decent bounty or Shay to occupy his attention, his mind was adrift in an ocean of endless reflection.

The Brownstone Agency was young. Functional bounty hunting was still limited to Trey at this point, but all the low-level bounties the police might be interested in shoving his way were being handled by the junior bounty hunter with ease.

Even if James *wanted* to go smack around some level-one or two bounties, he couldn't do much without disrupting Trey's momentum.

James turned off the machine and frowned down at the couch. A thin strip of fabric peeked out from underneath the piece of furniture, and he leaned over and tugged out the discovery.

The bounty hunter frowned and lifted his treasure: a pair of Shay's panties. "Huh. Why are *these* here?"

They'd had more than a little fun but it had been confined to the bedroom, making the couch panties a genuine mystery. He tossed around a few possibilities in his mind.

The simplest explanation was that Shay had gotten undressed in his living room when he wasn't paying attention, but more exotic explanations, such as magical teleporting panties, couldn't be completely dismissed.

James shrugged and marched into his bedroom with the underwear and then over to his dresser. He opened his special "Shay Drawer" to lay the panties out.

With that taken care of, he headed into his bathroom to pre-inspect the cleanliness level before he gathered supplies. Once he finished in the living room, it was his next mission. No man should ever attack something without having a little pre-mission intelligence. That always made the actual battle simpler.

He paused at the door, taking in the sink. One side was free of anything, but the other was almost a supermarket aisle, given the razor, shampoo, conditioner, makeup, and Shay's overly-elaborate crystal skull toothbrush holder.

"Probably some magical shit," James mumbled. "Ancient Atlantean anti-cavity magic or some shit."

The contrast on the sink was striking. All his toiletries had been put away in designated spots. Shay's side of the sink was a chaotic mess.

Not all that long ago there'd been no one in his space, but now he was domesticated, with a girlfriend and a daughter.

"Domestication isn't simple." He chuckled. "But it feels good."

James' phone rang from the living room, and he hurried there. Maybe some level five was tearing up the city and the police needed him to teach the man a lesson.

As he snatched the phone from the table, he smiled. It wasn't the police or Trey, but it *was* someone he wanted to talk to.

"Hey, Alison," James answered.

"Hey, Dad."

"Everything okay? No crazy Oriceran creatures messing with you? Or some big spell disaster?"

Alison laughed. "Everything's okay. No problems at all. Classes are going well, and things aren't all that different from last time. My energy sight is getting a lot better. I'm able to see stuff a lot more clearly now—not to mention the lie detection."

"That's handy," James rumbled. "You'll be able to see a lot more important stuff than most people."

"You know, I've been here a while now, but it's still kind of weird to think about how all my friends can do magic."

"Yeah, the only magic the average person has in LA is the ability to be rude in every situation." James frowned. "If everything is the same, why did you call?"

Alison sighed. "Because I worry about you when you're alone, and I know Aunt Shay is out of town."

The bounty hunter grunted. "I spent a long time alone before I met her or you. I know how to handle it."

"Just because you spent a long time alone doesn't mean it felt good."

A few seconds ticked by as James considered that. He couldn't deny the truth, even if the girl wasn't there to see his soul energy.

Shay and Alison filled a void in his soul he hadn't even realized was there. His days before had been simpler but shallower, and all the barbeque in Las Vegas wasn't enough to fill him with the satisfaction he felt now—not that he wouldn't have minded a bounty or two.

James cleared his throat. "Thanks, kid, but I'm really okay. Just trying to make sure everything is clean for when you come home."

"Home. I like the sound of that."

"Good, I want you to."

Alison laughed. "But I doubt you need to clean. I don't think you could let a place get dirty."

"It still gets dusty."

"You'd probably have a heart attack if you started looking at my room and bathroom too closely."

James chuckled. "I'm sure I could take it."

"Maybe."

They both laughed for a moment, then Alison sighed.

"Problem?" James inquired.

"There is something I guess I should tell you about."

"If there's a problem, just tell me and I'll handle it."

Alison let out a soft laugh. "It's not that kind of thing, Dad."

"What?"

James gritted his teeth. If Alison was being bullied at her magic school, he didn't care how many witches and wizards were teaching there. He'd kick in their damned gate and knock some damned respect into those punks.

"I had a boyfriend," Alison all but whispered.

"What?" James thundered. "A *boyfriend*? Who is it? I need their name, and you can tell them to expect a call from me."

The girl groaned. "That's the problem. Don't you see?"

"What? Is he not treating you right? I don't have any big bounties right now. I could fly there today for a little man-to-man with this little punk."

"I said I *had* a boyfriend, not that I *have* one."

James let out a little growl. "He dump you for some other girl? He thinks he's too good for you? I can still have a ta—"

"He dumped me because he's afraid of you, Dad," Alison snapped. "We'd only been going out for two days."

"Oh." He tried to sound contrite even as satisfaction filled him.

Alison let out a sigh. "He didn't know who my dad was when we started going out. It's not like we go around school constantly using our last names, you know? Then it came up in conversation, and he was all, 'Brownstone, like James Brownstone?' So I admitted you were my dad, and he freaked out and told me we had to break up."

"If he's that chickensh—" James took a deep breath. "If he's gonna run that easily, he's not the right one for you."

"I'm not looking for a husband yet, Dad. Just looking for a little fun."

"Just saying."

"And I'm just saying you're not helping. Try to be less intimidating next time you visit."

James could all but hear her glare through the phone.

"Sorry," he offered. "I know it probably sucks. I'd try and give you more advice, but I'm not exactly an expert when it comes to dating. Maybe Shay can give you a call when she gets back."

"No, I'm fine. I'm not really all that sad. It's not like I fell in love with a guy I was only dating for two days."

James resisted telling her how happy he was to hear that. Even if she wasn't all that upset about the break-up, she didn't need to hear her dad gloating about fucking with her love life from thousands of miles away.

"I promise to try and be less intimidating the next time I'm at the school."

"That's all I'm asking." A few beats of silence passed before Alison continued, "And I'm not all that mad or anything, Dad. I get that you're new at all this, and you're still a lot better dad than Walt ever was."

James chuckled darkly. All he had to do to be a better father than Walt Anderson was not sell Alison to gangsters —a low bar for sure. He'd still take the compliment.

"Thanks, kid. Can't wait to see you."

"I can't wait to see you either. I should get going, but I love you."

James smiled. All his tension faded with those simple words. "I love you, too, Alison."

That evening the bounty hunter marched up the walk to his church. The men associated with the simple stone church surrounded by huge ash trees had been responsible for so much, including raising him and making him into the man he was today.

They took an alien and made him a God-fearing human, even if they didn't know it. Someday they need to know the truth so the Vatican can reward them, especially for putting up with my ass.

On some days, he worried that the despair bug in Japan had been right and he'd been burdening Father McCartney too much, but for once his heart felt lighter. He'd gone a good week without killing anyone.

See, I'm already becoming a better man. A better human, even.

James made his way through the aisle separating the pews and toward the confessional booth. He slid the door open and stepped inside. The shadow of Father McCartney moved across the confessional screen as the priest took a seat.

The bounty hunter cleared his throat. "Bless me, Father, for I have sinned. It's been a week since my last confession, but on the plus side, I have very little to ask forgiveness for."

Father McCartney chuckled on the other side of the screen. "You'd be surprised at what God notices, my son, but please go on."

"The only bad thing I've done this week was beat up a

couple of rude, mealy-mouthed youths who tried to harass a woman."

The priest sighed. "I see. But you didn't kill them?"

"No. I just taught them a lesson."

"How hard did you beat them?"

James couldn't help but let a little chuckle escape. "I smacked them around a bit, but it was a lot less painful than them getting killed by the woman."

"I don't understand. This woman was dangerous?"

"She *can* be. Look, if you think about it, they came out ahead. I was almost doing them a favor." James shrugged.

"I'm concerned that you're associating with people so dangerous that you think beating someone up is a better solution than what they'd do."

"That's life, right?" James offered.

The priest sighed. "I suppose. Do ten Hail Marys later as penance and try and reflect on alternatives to violence, James."

"I will, Father." James turned toward the door but stopped. "I haven't had a chance to check lately. Is everything going well with the orphanage?"

"Oh, that? Yes, quite well." Surprise colored Father McCartney's voice. "Very well, in fact. In addition to all the money you've provided, we have a new benefactor."

"You do? That's good to hear."

"Yes. I must admit I'm surprised though. They are anonymous."

"Not everyone wants praise."

Father McCartney shifted on the other side of the screen. "You're saying it's not you?"

James shook his head. "Why would I play games like

that? Haven't I been straightforward with you about this the entire time?"

"I suppose you have. I also suppose I shouldn't be upset that a Good Samaritan wants to help the children. Perhaps you've inspired someone."

"Maybe."

"Have a good evening, my son."

"You too, Father." He slid the door open and stepped out of the confessional booth.

James waited until he was back in his truck before he pulled out his phone and sent a text:

Our gift to the church was received. I appreciate you handling the transfers. XOXO.

Lying to a priest in church might earn him a few frowns from the Big Man upstairs, but he was lying in the cause of helping the orphanage. That had to be at least worth a few points. Even after his earlier stock donation, the kids and the church still needed funds. If James had his way, he'd drown them in money enough to last until the Second Coming.

James started his F-350 and pulled away from the church, smiling. He'd always thought of himself a straight-forward man, but between the donations and smuggling an artifact from Seattle, he was proving to the world that James Brownstone could get you coming or going if you weren't careful.

His smile faded. Taking pride in making his life more complicated was a bad idea. The women in his life might be filling the hole in his soul, but damned if they weren't pulling him into some swamp of complicated living.

His phone chimed with a text from Shay.

Don't use shit like XOXO. You're not a teenage girl, and I'm betting even Alison doesn't do that.

"Yeah, women are the opposite of simple," he muttered under his breath.

Trey pushed into the Black Sun but lingered just inside the door as he took in the motley assortment of criminals and cops filling the place. Unease settled into his stomach; neutral ground was unnatural. In the end, a man had to pick a side. That was just the way the world worked.

Hell, *he* had. He had been a gangbanger before, and now he was a bounty hunter. When people blurred the lines too much, shit got messy and everyone was less satisfied.

But it didn't matter what he felt. The Black Sun was one of the most useful places to pick up info in LA. The owner and chief bartender Tyler might be a prick, but he was good at his job.

Time's gonna come, asshole, when you're gonna have to choose too. Make sure you pick the right side.

Trey jostled his way through the thick crowd and managed to find an empty stool at the bar. Tyler set a glass in front of him seconds later.

"A Manhattan, as usual," the bartender explained with a smile.

"You're a good bartender, I'll give you that."

"But not a good man?"

Trey snorted but didn't say anything. If there was one thing he'd learned about Tyler, the man was obsessed with respect—even more than Trey was.

Modulating his speech a little so as not to disrespect the bar owner would go a long way toward keeping him as a contact.

The junior bounty hunter had even considered dropping his gangster accent, but with that many criminals around, including the occasional gang member associated with his old enemies, it was a bad idea. Sometimes the mask needed to stay up.

"Ain't no one a good man," Trey replied. He took a sip of his Manhattan. "Not in the end."

"Damn right." Tyler stared at the other man for a moment and shook his head. "I don't know what to do with you."

"You gave me a drink. That's all you need to do."

The bartender shook his head. "No, it's not that simple. You see, on the one hand I respected what you were doing as a gang leader. You carved out a little space of your own, made a little money. Even managed to keep Brownstone from coming down on you. But now..." He gestured toward Trey.

"Now what?"

"Now you're not a gang leader anymore. You've traded in your colors for a suit and working for that asshole Brownstone. I can't respect that."

Trey took another drink of his Manhattan. "So what's that mean, Tyler? We gonna have an issue?"

"I'm not Brownstone. I don't cause trouble for people who don't cause me trouble. Not only that, you're connected to not just him now, but also the cops, so fucking with you might cause me trouble."

Trey snorted. "You know, today I ain't here for anything

but a drink. Maybe I need to go to a place that don't judge me."

"What's that mean? Like where?"

Trey shrugged. "Shit, I don't know. Maybe some bar run by the motherfucking Ku Klux Klan."

Tyler winced. "That hurt, Trey. Whatever." He shook his head. "The drink's on me." The bartender headed toward the opposite end of the bar, muttering under his breath.

Bitch, please. You wouldn't even have all your fancy new tables if it wasn't for James.

The bounty hunter gulped down his drink and wiped his mouth with his sleeve. His phone beeped.

The police had earmarked a level-two bounty for him, which meant the man most likely had special value as a witness. The quicker he was captured, the better.

Guess you're right, Tyler. I'm not what I was. But we all have to choose a side in the end.

5

Dina hugged her legs to her chest and cried. Her daddy was dead, and Red Eyes had gotten away. The policemen had promised they'd do something, but they couldn't win—not against a monster. Red Eyes had even told her so.

A policeman couldn't kill a monster. They'd just die, too. She needed a magical knight like the one she'd seen in her favorite show, *Brave Adventures of the Oriceran Princess.*

The girl forced her crying down to mere sniffles. She needed to be strong for her daddy.

Dina hopped out of the cracked plastic chair in the sterile white room where the nice lady from Child Protective Services had told her to wait and picked up the remote control from the woman's desk. She started flipping through the channels, and she'd gone through five when she stopped.

An image of a muscular man with a strange face dominated the screen. He was kind of ugly when she thought about it, with ridges and odd patterns all over his face.

"Class-six bounty hunter James Brownstone has been taking down the most dangerous bounties for years, but in this last year has gained fame for several high-profile bounty takedowns and his one-man war against the now-defunct Japanese criminal syndicate known as the Harriken."

An old man in glasses who looked constipated appeared on the screen.

"We asked criminology expert Dr. Tasker from UNLV to give us his insights into this now-famous, or depending on who you ask, *infamous* man."

Dr. Tasker cleared his throat. "The problem, you see, is that our entire society... No, our entire *civilization*, really, arose in a context where magic wasn't that common, or at least not acknowledged. We're still grappling with how to handle magical threats. Our laws and, quite frankly, law enforcement is inadequate for the task. Men like James Brownstone fill the gap. I'm sure in a decade or two more this will all smooth itself out, but if we didn't have bounty hunters right now, society would quickly be overwhelmed by magical criminals."

Dina couldn't understand everything the old man had said, but she understood that James Brownstone went after magical bad guys.

She'd found her knight.

The door opened, and the woman from Child Protective Services entered. She looked at the television and frowned.

"Sweetie, you shouldn't be watching something like that." She turned the television off.

"You know James Brownstone?"

"James Brownstone? The bounty hunter?" The woman shrugged. "I've heard of him. He's famous."

Dina pointed to the television. "An old man on TV said Mr. Brownstone takes down magical bad guys."

"He is a high-level bounty hunter, so, yes, I guess that's what he does." An uncomfortable look passed over the woman's face.

"You should call Mr. Brownstone to get Red Eyes."

The woman sighed and shook her head. "They don't have a bounty out on the man who killed your father."

"Wasn't a man. Was a monster."

"Of course he was, sweetie."

Dina could tell the woman didn't believe her.

The woman sighed before continuing, "The point is, men like James Brownstone... Well, he's not a hero. He does it for money, and until they're a high-level bounty, he won't care. He doesn't even live in Las Vegas. He lives in Los Angeles. That's far away, sweetie."

Dina stuck out her lip and nodded. She didn't understand why the woman wouldn't help her call Mr. Brownstone, but it didn't matter. She'd found her magical knight, and she'd bring him to Las Vegas somehow to kill Red Eyes no matter what it took.

Charlyce watched the front door of the building from across the street. No one paid much attention to the homeless woman as they walked past.

No one spoke to her or even turned their head her way. They didn't want to see her. It'd make them too uncomfortable.

She was counting on it. Sometimes invisibility had its advantages.

Lieutenant Maria Hall was used to two things: getting what she wanted and yelling at people. She wasn't as used to being on the receiving end.

The chief of police shook his phone in his hand. "Do you know what the report says, Lieutenant?"

"That we took down a dangerous magical threat, who, if left unchecked, could have killed or injured hundreds of people?"

The chief narrowed his eyes. "Twenty-four million dollars. You blew through twenty-four million dollars in seven minutes. How the hell are we supposed to pay for all of that?"

Maria crossed her arms. "AET was just supposed to let some dangerous threat wander through the city?"

"I read the report. You initiated the contact based on some anonymous tip. For all we know, some punk kid was trying to swat some witch because she beat them at some stupid video game."

"With all due respect, sir, we didn't fire until she attacked us. If she had been an innocent woman, that wouldn't have happened. Not only that, but the evidence ties this woman to multiple murders on the East Coast. Interpol's even getting involved now, saying she might be linked to other deaths in Europe. This wasn't some random witch walking in the park. That was a magical hitman we took down." Maria shot out of her chair. "Not only that, but this woman was linked to Brownstone. You're bitching to me about a few million dollars here and there? What about *that* guy? How much damage has been caused in this city because of him going after people or vice versa?"

The chief pointed to her chair. "Sit down, Lieutenant. Now."

Maria dropped back into her seat with a frown. "Brownstone's the problem, sir. You should bill him. It was *his* floozy."

"That's another thing." The chief set his phone down and shook his head. "You need to get the fuck over Brownstone. You can't blame him for everything, and your own follow-up report talks about how you wasted even more money to use a rare artifact to question him about this woman, and... Well, refresh my memory, Lieutenant. Did you detect any lies from Brownstone about this woman?"

"He was tricking us somehow. Maybe he had some sort of lying spell."

"Oh, so he conveniently had that magic prepared in case you showed up with a rare and expensive artifact we don't use in routine investigations?"

Maria groaned. "I'm telling you he's connected to that woman. We linked her to the airport incident."

"We're cops. We go off evidence, not vendettas. I don't want to see or hear anything about Brownstone again from you unless you personally witness him committing a major felony." He held up a hand. "And, no, beating up or killing a valid bounty doesn't count."

Maria opened her mouth to offer another rebuttal but shut it when the chief's phone rang.

He snatched it up with a frown. "What? I thought I told you I'd be busy." His face twitched, and he sighed. "I'm sorry, Mr. Mayor. Yes. Yes. I understand." He glanced at Lieutenant Hall. "Right, I'll tell her. Yes, I happen to be speaking with her right now on the subject." He adjusted the phone. "Yes, I'll let her know the details. Thank you for letting me know." The chief placed the phone face down on his desk.

The AET officer just waited for the chief to deliver whatever news he'd received from the mayor. His fading anger suggested something big.

"The Oriceran consulate, on behalf of several local Oriceran leaders, has just contacted the mayor. They are concerned that the use of heavy magic toward the police in the most recent incident will reflect negatively on Oricerans."

"What the fuck do they care? She wasn't Oriceran, just an Earth witch, it looks like."

The chief snorted. "They care enough that they're willing to cover the costs involved in controlling the incident and throw in a little extra for the AET budget. They stressed to the mayor that they are concerned with out-of-control magic. According to them, they understand how bad these situations can get and want to do what they can to help smooth things out locally and help promote the authorities keeping irresponsible magic users in check."

Maria grinned. "Hell, at least *someone* understands that

importance of what we do. Too bad it has to be a bunch of people from another planet."

The chief waved her away with a snort. "You did your job, and now a bunch of elves, dwarves, and who knows what else are cleaning up for you. Stop smiling, stop blaming Brownstone for things, and get the hell out of my office."

The lieutenant stood and waved. She made it to the door before the snark bubbled out.

"Okay, sure, I won't blame Brownstone, but that means he gets no credit for any of this!"

Hannah glared at her father as they continued into the dark alley. "This better not be a trick."

Her father shrugged with a grin. "What's the trick?"

"You told me you were gonna scare me on purpose to see if I had learned to be brave this year."

He laughed. "Yeah. You're going into second-grade next year. You're practically an adult."

Hannah squinted as glowing red eyes appeared in the darkness and grabbed her dad's arm. "This isn't funny, Dad."

He frowned and glared into the shadows. "It's okay, honey. I got this." He nodded. "Hey, whoever is there, you better turn around if you know what's good for you."

"What's good for me?" replied a hollow voice.

Her father reached underneath his jacket and pulled out a gun.

Hannah gasped. "You brought a gun?"

"I bring a gun everywhere now." He pointed the weapon into the darkness. "Lots of freaks in Vegas. I told you about how my buddy got mugged a few months ago. Never can be too safe, honey."

"Let's just go and call the police, Dad."

Laughter bubbled up from the darkness. "A gun? Police? Both useless."

"Yeah, asshole," Hannah's father growled. "Turn around and run, or you're going to end up with some lead in your head."

Hannah trembled beside him and gripped his arm tightly. "Let's just get out of here. Please."

"Shoot me now," the voice called from the shadows. "This is your one chance. You'll fail, but at least it's a chance."

"Shut your mouth," Hannah's father shouted, then swallowed. "Okay, honey, I think you need to head back toward the street while I *talk* with this guy."

"Dad, I'm scared," the girl whispered.

The outline of the figure grew closer.

"Last chance," the girl's father barked. "I'm warning you."

"I gave you your chance," came the hollow and raspy response. "Now you die."

Hannah's father pulled the trigger twice in rapid succession. His daughter screamed and put her hands over her ears.

The figure didn't fall. He burst toward them, the shadows cloaking almost every feature except his red eyes. His arm contorted in the darkness, and his fingers bent and twisted until the outline of a sharp blade cut through the shadows.

"What the fuck?" Hannah's father yelled. He kept firing into the figure until his gun clicked empty. The rough outline of his target remained hidden, and the man didn't fall or give the slightest indication he'd been hit.

Hannah, tears streaming down her face, backed up. "No, no, no. This isn't happening. *This isn't happening.* This isn't real."

A mottled leathery arm emerged from the darkness. The sharp blade wasn't a weapon, or at least not a conventional one. It was a thin bony protrusion. Hannah continued backing up until she bumped into a wall, then stood there hyperventilating.

The young girl closed her eyes and fell to the ground, covering her face with her hands.

Her daddy cried out and his gun clattered against the ground, and there was a dull thud a second later. Hannah risked opening her eyes, and she screamed.

Her father still gripped the gun, but the hand holding it now lay on the ground, detached at the wrist. His open, lifeless eyes stared at her from his severed head.

The red-eyed figure retreated into the shadows. "Go ahead and run, little angel."

Hannah forced herself to her feet despite her shaking knees and chattering teeth. She tried to will her feet to move, but they remained stubbornly stationary. She sobbed, and her salty tears kept her from making out anything but the red glow.

"Run now," the voice growled. "It's better that they

know. Better that they hear it from you. You can go ahead and tell everyone that I am the one who makes angels cry."

The girl stumbled as she ran, but picked herself up and continued running down the alley. The mocking laughter of the killer followed her.

6

"I'm out of shit to clean," James mumbled. "Fuck."

The tile gleamed, and the carpet looked even better than when it'd been installed, which had only been a few days ago in any case. Even the slightest hint of dirt in the grout had fallen prey to his attention. There was no dirty laundry or suspicious-smelling food. He'd even trimmed all the bushes in his yard and made sure his lawn was even.

Everything was clean, organized, and in its place. Everything was...simple as long as he didn't go into the bathroom.

None of that helped him figure out how he was going to fill the rest of the day.

James frowned and shook his head. It wasn't like he'd never taken a few days off bounty hunting before, so he didn't understand why this gaping chasm lingered in his soul. Confession had helped but hadn't closed it. He was missing something, but he wasn't sure what.

When he stepped into his room and looked at his

dresser, he knew *exactly* what he was missing—or more accurately, who.

Shay and Alison.

James sighed. Loneliness. He'd always been on the outside of society, but he'd never felt the painful void accompanying true loneliness.

Shay needs to concentrate on her job and Alison on school. I can't call them like an emo teenage girl.

The bounty hunter grunted. He also couldn't sit around his house all day. Maybe a drink at the Leanan Sídhe was a good plan.

He tossed that idea after a few seconds. The problem was that anytime he hit a crowded place, people swarmed him to ask questions or ask for his fucking autograph. Walking into the popular Irish pub might put him around people, but it'd also mean he wouldn't have two seconds to think.

Not only that, he stilled owed the Professor participation in a Bard of Filth competition. He might be able to tolerate the pain with Shay around, but not by himself.

So where could he go? What could he do? What could possibly fill the deep chasm in his heart?

A wide grin spread across his face. There was one constant in his life, something he could claim as one of his earliest loves.

It was time to get some barbeque. And not just any barbeque, the best damned barbeque on the planet.

"Jessie Rae's," James rumbled. He grabbed his coat and made a quick trip to his basement to secure a .45. While he didn't expect any trouble on his way to Las Vegas, he also hadn't expected any trouble at the Italian restaurant. Being properly prepared would mean fewer regrets later.

Maybe a few knives. Just in case. A grenade wouldn't hurt. Just one.

Now armed better than the average man but carrying far less than was typical for him or Shay, the bounty hunter made his way to his truck. He started up the F-350, smiling at the fact he'd filled the gas tank the night before. He wouldn't even have to stop on his way to Las Vegas.

James pulled out his phone, synced it with his truck's speakers, and turned on the *Sauce Wars* podcast, then headed out.

He half-listened to the hosts' chatter as his mind drifted to the growing labyrinth of complicated relationships now defining his life. He had a girlfriend. Well, a lover. Hell, he wasn't even sure what he should call her.

He had a daughter. For that matter, he had friends like Mack and Trey and a pile of employees.

Simple was gone. No, not just gone. Simple was *dead*, its body blown into bits by a rocket launcher over the ocean.

Keep It Simple, Stupid. James had lived his life by that philosophy, but without sacrificing every connection he now had it was no longer possible. Even if he'd left behind the woman and girl who had a claim on his heart, his reputation followed him everywhere.

There was no keeping it simple when you were the Scourge of Harriken.

James grunted. None of it mattered, anyway. If some genie popped out of one of Shay's artifacts and offered him the chance to turn back time, he'd tell him to stuff his ass back in the bottle.

He pulled his truck onto the highway.

Fuck it. If I wouldn't change anything, no use overthinking it. I might not be able to keep it simple, but I can at least keep it from getting more *complicated.*

Trey adjusted his tie and smiled into the camera. He was taking far too much satisfaction in standing in front of a police station for his interview.

The reporter standing next to him had a nice rack. Maybe he'd ask her out after they finished.

"This is Nina Edgars, with an exclusive interview with a man whose name has been coming up a lot lately—Trey Garfield, a bounty hunter with the newly formed Brownstone Agency." She stuck the microphone in his face. "Can you tell us a little bit about the bounty you just captured?"

Trey gave the woman and the camera a bright smile. This situation called for Smooth Trey, not Gangster Trey. He was glad he had on one of his more dapper suits.

"Sure, Nina. Today wasn't a big deal. We weren't talking about King Pyro here." He chuckled, and the reporter joined him. "Not to say that the man I brought in, Anatoly Egorov, wasn't dangerous. He's a level-two bounty. My boy's been traveling up and down the West Coast killing people for cash, so I brought him in for a little cash of my own."

Nina nodded. "And you're not concerned about vengeance?"

"By the time Anatoly gets out of jail, I hope to be retired on some tropical island somewhere."

They shared another laugh.

"Mr. Garfield, please give us a little insight into how you tracked the elusive hitman down."

"Not so hard. I've got a lot of contacts on the street. The thing is, no one can disappear—not really. A man shows up in town, he sends out ripples. All you have to do is look for them. Even if someone doesn't want to give up a name, you can tell if a certain guy is fidgeting more or people are avoiding a certain bar...that sort of thing."

"Very impressive." A hungry look appeared on Nina's face.

Shit. Down, girl.

"Isn't it true that before you were a bounty hunter, you were a criminal?"

Trey kept his smile. "I used to lead a collective neighborhood security association if that's what you're talking about."

"Is that how you referred to your street gang?"

"It's all perspective, Nina. I'll only note that a man like me knows the streets and what to look for, like those ripples I mentioned. It helps me bring in the dangerous guys before they hurt innocent people."

The hungry gleam in the woman's eyes only intensified. "That's an interesting perspective, and your reputation so far is one of extreme professionalism."

"We at the Brownstone Agency strive for that, even when dealing with hitmen."

"Even though your boss is a killer?"

Trey couldn't help the frown that broke through. "Excuse me?"

"James Brownstone, the founder of your agency. He's killed a number of his bounties."

Trey forced the smile back onto his face. "Mr. Brownstone has defended himself on numerous occasions against very dangerous men. Considering he normally only deals with level-three and above bounties, you're almost always talking about not just criminals, but criminals with magic. You think Mr. Brownstone should have exercised restraint against the necromancer body-hopper in Detroit?"

Nina's face twitched. "And the Harriken?"

Trey laughed. "Last time I checked, they had a dead-or-alive organizational bounty on them. The police helped block off the street while he took them down."

"Are you willing to guarantee that every death associated with James Brownstone was legal and justified?"

Trey snorted. "Nina, I can't guarantee that everything you've done in your life is legal and justified."

The reporter frowned. "So you have nothing you want to add about James Brownstone?"

"Add about Brownstone? Sure. This city and country are safer because he's around." Trey shrugged. "Mexico's safer because he's around. He's taken down more than a few big bounties down there, too. Japan's also safer because of him."

Nina turned to the camera. "There you have it. Trey Garfield of the Brownstone Agency providing some interesting perspective on his controversial boss."

The cameraman lowered his equipment, and the reporter stormed off without further comment.

"Not like I would have asked you out anyway after you tried to do James like that," Trey mumbled.

The pile of stripped ribs spoke of both James' hunger and the quality of the cuisine. He'd wanted to slow himself down and savor the glories of Jessie Rae's God Sauce as it rested on his tongue, but his self-control had failed as soon as the first rib had hit his mouth. Several pounds of ribs later he didn't regret his choice, and he was confident he wouldn't after several more.

An older couple sitting at one of the other tables looked between James and the wall several times before the wife cleared her throat.

"Excuse me, sir, but would you happen to be James Brownstone?"

He shrugged. "Last time I checked."

"Honey, come over here. It's James Brownstone." She pointed to a picture on the wall. "Just like in the picture."

The picture hanging on the wall depicted James standing next to Mike, the owner of Jessie Rae's. It had been James' first attempt at a barbeque competition. He had come in first, but he attributed that more to Mike helping him than any skill of his own.

A rumbling chuckle escaped. He'd assumed the couple recognized him from his bounty-hunting exploits. It had never even occurred to him that someone might recognize him for barbeque.

The woman's husband hurried over to the table and extended a bony hand. James shook it, and the couple seated themselves at his table.

"Maybe you can settle a debate," the husband began, "between my wife and me about barbeque."

James shrugged. "I can offer an opinion. Maybe a stupid one."

The couple exchanged a glance before the husband spoke again. "Is there one type of meat that's better than the others?"

James shook his head. "Not really. Doesn't matter what type of meat, or even the cut. Different types of meats and cuts work for different meals. That's how barbeque is special."

The wife pointed to a television in the corner. "Look, Mr. Brownstone. You're on television. Did you win another competition?"

He shook his head. "Nope, haven't been in one for a while."

The sound was off, but he could read the subtitles with ease. A local Vegas station was rerunning a report from a sister affiliate in LA.

James watched stone-faced as Nina Edgars interviewed Trey. The reporter trying to paint him in a bad light was only a mild annoyance, which watching his friend defend him more than made up for.

"Oh, wow," the wife commented as the report ended. "I didn't realize you were a famous bounty hunter, too. Do you do that in-between the barbeque competitions?"

He laughed.

Charlyce stared at the row of televisions behind the shop window, all of them set to the interview. She blinked several times as the well-dressed bounty hunter discussed his recent bounty and defended his boss James Brownstone.

"That can't be him." She shook her head. "But it ain't like there's that many Trey Garfields in LA who look like that. He's got the same face, even if he's a man now." She turned from the window and made her way up the street.

It'd been years since she'd last talked to her nephew. She didn't *deserve* to talk to him; not really.

But I need your help, Trey. I need you to get me to James Brownstone.

He was the only man who could help her little angel now.

7

Trey had just pulled his F-350 into the parking lot of his nana's house when his phone rang.

"Another of my adoring public."

It felt like every random woman he'd ever dated or man he'd talked to for five minutes in his entire life had called him since the interview had played. Everyone wanted a piece of Trey Garfield now, or at least a loan from him.

"Not like I'm rich, you leeches," he mumbled to himself as he raised the phone.

Trey frowned. The caller ID didn't reveal anything other than the origination city: Las Vegas, Nevada. He didn't know anyone in Las Vegas. He'd never left California in his entire life. The phone continued to ring as he debated answering it.

"Whatever. Probably just some bookie looking to score off me like Tyler does off James." He lifted the phone to his face. "This is Trey. What do you got for me?"

A surprised gasp came over the line.

"Who is this?" he pressed.

"I… It's been in a while, Trey."

He narrowed his eyes. The voice sounded familiar, but he couldn't place it.

"Who is this?" he demanded.

A long sigh followed. "Aunt Charlyce."

"What the fuck? Auntie Charlyce? You…" He pulled the phone back to stare at it as if he could see her on the other end. He didn't want to believe it, but it did sound like the woman he remembered. "Nana told me you disappeared. I figured she was just being nice and didn't want to tell me you drank yourself to death."

"I ain't proud of who I was, and I ain't proud of who I fell in with. Not only the booze took me. The Devil's needle also took me for a while, and I lost myself. I don't blame anyone but myself for that. I wasn't strong enough, and I hurt you and everyone."

"Whatever. At least you ain't my mother. She took off, and she didn't have an excuse."

"That's all in the past. We can move forward now."

Trey snorted. "So my junkie auntie is calling me up now? What, you need some money so you can score some drugs? I ain't playing that shit. You want to shoot up or snort dust, you scrounge your own fucking money."

"No, it ain't like that. I found forgiveness. I found Jesus, and I quit the drugs and the booze. I'm clean and sober, I swear."

"Clean and sober for how long? Since you saw me on TV last night?"

The woman sighed over the line. "A month. I'm saving up money, trying to get back on my feet—I swear to the Lord in heaven. I'm not proud of what I've become, but I know now that part of helping myself means helping others. When I ran to drugs, it was because I didn't care about no one but myself. Now I have a chance to really help someone else."

"So you want money from me after all? So you can help some other junkies?" Trey scoffed. "Everyone wants a piece of me now, but they didn't give a shit when I was trying to push my way out of the ghetto. The only people who ever really gave a shit were Nana and James Brownstone. So, no, you can't have my money. I don't care if you're blood."

"It ain't like that. I don't want money."

"Then why the fuck are you calling me after seven years?" Trey barked.

"You just said it yourself...James Brownstone. I've read about him. He's a good man. Blessed by God."

"Blessed by God? He *is* a badass, so I wouldn't put it past him."

"I read about how he's a religious man. He goes to church."

Trey sighed. "So, what, it ain't enough for you to try and get money from me? You going straight to the big man? Is that it? Mr. Brownstone don't put up with motherfucking disrespect."

"You don't understand!" Charlyce hissed. "Something evil's walking in Las Vegas," she whispered. "Not natural. Not even Oriceran. I read on the internet about how Mr. Brownstone has stopped not just evil men, but evil monsters. That's what I need—a man blessed by God to help fight the evil."

"Listen to this cracked-out bullshit! You expect me to

believe any of this?" Trey all but shouted. "How do I know you ain't high right now?"

"You can read about it in the news, about the little girl who lost her father. How his head was cut off and his body cut up. It's evil. A demon, I tell you. We got that hole in the worlds now. The Oricerans can come through it, but who's to say that Satan's minions can't, too? It's a dark time, which is why we need men like Mr. Brownstone and men like you. The police can't cope, not by themselves."

Trey blew out a breath as he thought over everything she was saying. He barely paid attention to anything that happened outside of Los Angeles County. If some magical creature was wandering around Las Vegas, it could easily be a level-four or five bounty and the big man might be interested.

Hell, the big man might be *needed*.

"Fine," Trey muttered. "I'm gonna double-check your story, and to do that I'll need to meet with you in Vegas."

"I know both your mother and me done you wrong, and I'm glad Mama steered you right."

"I ain't so much as looking at the big man's number until I've met you and double-checked your story. I'll call you when I get there."

"Bless you, Trey," the woman replied, her voice wavering. "Bless you."

He ended the call and stared the phone for a long while before shaking his head. "This shit is dumb. I'm getting hustled by my own flesh and blood."

Trey shook his head and texted James. He didn't need to bother the big man with his aunt's bullshit yet, but the man was still his boss and needed to know where he was.

I have to go to Vegas for a day or two. No bounties from the 5-0 in the pipe.

He started up his truck and pulled on the street. Minutes later, his phone chimed with a text.

Vegas? You should stop by Jessie Rae's and get some barbeque then.

Trey chuckled. "Always with the motherfucking barbeque. I wonder what's he up to right now. Probably chilling in his new house, thinking about how badass he is."

Charlyce passed through the alley, nodding to a few of the other regulars. "Hey, Mildred. Hey, Bobby."

"Hey, Charlyce," Bobby replied with a wave.

Mildred finished tying up a plastic bag in her shopping cart. "I haven't seen you around here much lately."

"Been hitting cans in different territory. Trying to save up some money, you know. I was wondering, though, if you could help me out."

"I ain't got any money. If I did I wouldn't live on the street now, would I?"

Bobby and Mildred both laughed.

Charlyce shook her head. "I don't want no money from you, but I was just trying to figure out a good place to get a shower and some clothes."

"Shower and some clothes?" Bobby eyed her. "You looking to get a job? Don't bother. They ask you for a permanent address, and if you give 'em a homeless shelter's they won't hire you. It's why I gave up even looking."

"Not a job. Not yet, anyway." Charlyce sighed. "My

nephew is coming to meet me. I haven't seen him in seven years. Last he saw me I wasn't…a good woman, so he ain't expecting much from me."

Bobby and Mildred both gave sage nods.

"Maybe you should sell that phone," Bobby offered.

Charlyce shook her head. "Priorities. This phone is what's gonna let me get a job and get back into regular society. You ain't nothing without the internet. I need this phone for my future."

"They have a shower down at the rescue mission," Mildred suggested. "They might have some clothes you could have, too. If you got any money at all, you could try St. Vincent's. They sell stuff real cheap there."

"Thanks. I'll check them out." Charlyce shook her head. "I gotta do this, but I'd be lyin' if I said I ain't scared."

"Don't worry about it. If it's meant to be, it'll be."

"You ever meet any of your family?"

Bobby shrugged.

Mildred shook her head. "I haven't seen any of them for twenty years. Seven years ain't so bad." She smiled. "Good luck. If you can kick the needle and the bottle, you can handle a little meeting with your family."

Bobby nodded his agreement.

Charlyce offered them both a smile. She could never have a future if she didn't face her past, and her angel needed the help. She might not be strong enough to face down the kind of evil that now stalked Las Vegas, but at least she could find the man who could.

Detective Lafayette stared at the report on the computer and shook his head. Their killer was stepping up his game —three murders in less than a week. They'd thought they had the beginning of a pattern, only male adult victims in the presence of children. The most recent murder victims broke part of the pattern with both a mother and a father targeted, but it didn't change the fact their suspect appeared to be targeting parents.

He leaned back in his chair and let out a long sigh. "How reliable is the witness testimony of a traumatized four-year-old, a seven-year-old, and a five-year-old?"

His partner Detective West shrugged. "Look, we've got three deaths now, similar MO—decapitation and mutilation. Two in alleys and one in a parking lot. It's not like those little girls impaled and sliced up their parents."

"Yeah, I'm not saying that, but the other shit?"

"They've all said the same thing—some weird shadow shit with red glowing eyes. Even if the last two kids heard about the mutilation on TV, we haven't released anything to the public about the red glowing eyes. You telling me three little kids came up with the same details?" Detective West snorted. "And all three of those kids mentioned the killer talking about them being angels. Tell me they all made that up! It's amazing they are still fucking sane after what they saw."

Detective Lafayette ran his hands through his hair. "*Fuck.* You know what this means, don't you?"

"Yeah. We can't deny it now. It's magical shit. If we can find the suspect, we can point AET at him and let them do their thing, but the fucker's not exactly easy to pin down. And for all we know, he could be teleporting around."

Detective West glanced at a map hanging on the wall. They'd placed pins marking the murder sites. They didn't cluster in a single area; they were several miles apart each. It was too damned large an area to canvass even if they grabbed every last officer in the Las Vegas Metropolitan Police Department.

"We've got another option," Detective Lafayette suggested.

"What, wait until this fucker kills half the parents in Vegas? Or until he decides he wants to follow-up on the kids, too? He only didn't kill the first one because he couldn't get to her. He's left the last couple alone, but how long is that going to last?"

"We've got an MO, and we've got a rough description."

His partner laughed. "Shadow monster with a transforming bone arm, tentacles, and red glowing eyes? We're not going to get within the same time zone as a search warrant with something like that, and that's if we even knew where to search."

"Yeah, but it's enough to get a bounty going."

Detective West shook his head. "With what money? Our budget's tighter than ever, and we've just started investigating. The city won't even begin to touch reserve funds until everything's more solid, and the feds are still pissed at us about the last incident. We're not going to get any decent bounty hunters with piddly cash."

Detective Lafayette nodded. "Look, I say we hit up the Nevada Resort Association. The first kill was close to the Strip. The last thing any casino owner wants around here is people spooked about a serial killer. I say we go so far as to tell 'em we're going to aggressively talk about it in the news if they don't cough up some cash."

"You want to extort money out of casino and resort owners?"

"It's not extortion. It's protection, and for their own good." Detective Lafayette shrugged.

Detective West laughed. "That's what the mobsters always say."

8

James stifled a yawn as he pulled into the hotel parking lot. He'd been planning to head back to LA, but the text from Trey had changed his mind. The junior bounty hunter had never left California as far as James knew, and out of nowhere he was suddenly going to Vegas? Something smelled off, and Trey might need a little back-up. Trusting a man and ignoring that he might need help were two separate things.

Not hitting the road for another long stretch wasn't such a bad thing either. As glorious as Jessie Rae's barbeque was, it didn't stop James from needing rest.

He stepped out of his truck and headed toward the hotel lobby.

I need to play this shit right. I don't want Trey thinking I don't trust him. This might have nothing to do with the job, but I still want to be here if he needs a little extra muscle.

The hotel doors slid open, and James made his way to the front desk. The faded carpets and cracked paint proved the place wasn't a five-star resort, but there were no junkies shooting up outside or gunfire in the background. James just needed a place to sleep where no one would try to mug him in the middle of the night.

The manager stepped out of a back office and looked James up and down as he ran a hand through his too-slick hair. "You need a room?"

"Yeah," James rumbled.

"How long, big man? We don't do day-to-day here."

The bounty hunter frowned, unsure how long Trey might need him. "About a week?"

The manager chuckled. "Don't sound so sure. Okay, I'll check you in, but you've got to give your cancellation notice within forty-eight hours. Otherwise, we're still charging you for the day."

"That's fine."

It wasn't like the price of this hotel was going to make or break James. He probably spent more money on supplies for his average firefight than he'd spend paying for a week at the hotel. He fiddled around in his wallet for a credit card.

The manager nodded to himself as if he'd just made a decision. "Hey, you looking for a free week?"

James looked up. "Huh? What are you talking about?"

"I'm looking for some new security. You're a big piece of meat, fella, and you would scare away the riffraff. You sign up, I'll comp you for the week, and then we can hit hourly after that. Plus, you get a free continental breakfast."

The bounty hunter chuckled. "Sorry, pal. I've already got a job."

Disappointment showed on the man's face. "Fair enough. Just keep it in mind."

Ten minutes later James sat on the bed in Room 202, wondering what the hell he'd even do if Trey didn't call for help. He'd need to stay a day or two just in case, but it wasn't like he could spend all day eating at Jessie Rae's, and he had even less to do in Las Vegas than he did in Los Angeles.

Maybe I should go on a road trip for a few days and clear out my head.

James leaned over and picked up a few fliers from the nightstand. Las Vegas wasn't some tiny village. There had to be *something* interesting to do that didn't involve kicking ass or barbeque.

"True passion comes with music," he read, staring at a picture of a woman in a sequined gown being twirled by a suited man. "Learn how to dance." He set the flier down.

Does Shay like that kind of thing? Sometimes she likes fancy and sometimes she doesn't. Maybe I'll ask her when she gets back.

James tossed the flier back on the nightstand and sighed. He'd never, ever worried about learning how to dance before. He didn't regret starting something with Shay, but it was occasionally hard not to lament the loss of his simpler existence.

"They could change my nickname to the Dancing Ghost." He chuckled.

His stomach rumbled, and he thumbed through some of the other fliers, looking for somewhere decent to eat. He stopped on a picture of a huge juicy burger. An In-N-Out burger was only a mile away, all but begging for a walking excursion.

A little exercise and a snack sounded perfect. He eyed his phone again, wondering if he should contact Trey and ask him what was going on before shaking his head.

"Burger first, worry later."

Detective Lafayette moved the mouse and clicked on several of the drop-down boxes to examine the options. He shook his head.

"Damn, this is complicated. Have you ever set one of these up before, West?"

The other detective nodded. "Yeah, a few times before I was transferred to homicide. Why?"

"Look at some of these options." Detective Lafayette pointed to the screen. "Option 2B: Please define if the bounty can be classified as living or dead. What the fuck does that mean? Who puts a bounty on a dead guy?" He shook his head. "Guess that brings new meaning to a dead-or-alive bounty."

"Don't you remember that zombie dude they had to put down a few years back? I mean, technically he was dead, even if he kept moving until they blew him up. It's supposed to be about setting expectations."

The other detective sighed. "Fucking Oriceran. Someone should figure out how to slam the gates closed and get rid of magic again." His attention flicked to a line near the top of the screen: **PROJECTED BOUNTY: LEVEL ONE**. "We need serious help, and that's going to be at least level three or higher."

Detective West shrugged. "Look, we've got the red

glowing eyes and the deaths, along with the shapeshifting, so we've got a murderer with at least some magical capability. As long as we enter all that shit, we'll get at least a level three easily."

"Yeah, I guess you got a point."

Detective Lafayette spent a few moments selecting options and entering information before speaking again. "The second witness said her dad unloaded into the killer. Given the recovered gun and the shell casings, we've got reason to think she wasn't wrong or exaggerating, which means our boy may be resistant to small-arms fire. That's got be worth something."

The other man shook his head. "That still might not be enough to get him to level four. Remember that bastard last year? They said even though you could shoot the fucker at point-blank range and he wouldn't die, he was still only level three because he wasn't that strong or fast or anything."

"What about that shadow shit?" Detective Lafayette furrowed his brow. "So we've got… Where's the box? Ah, there it is. Unidentified Sensory Manipulation, One or More Senses." He selected that option and then "Physical Resistance: Small Arms Fire."

PROJECTED BOUNTY: LEVEL FOUR.

The two cops nodded to each other, satisfied smiles on their faces. Arresting the man would be best, but they had the citizens of Las Vegas to protect. A tough bounty-hunter or two might be able to follow up on different leads denied the police.

Detective Lafayette clicked around some of the other

options. "Anything you can think of so we can scare up a level five?"

Detective West shrugged. "I don't think so. He's got no mass kill skills, and we have no idea if he can…" He leaned over to look at the screen, "summon or control non-terrestrial entities or previously non-animate constructs."

"What the fuck does *that* mean?"

"If the asshole can summon spirits or ghosts or create zombies, that sort of thing. It's hard to get to level five without a guy being able to blow up half a city by himself or make an army, or fuck harder with the laws of physics than your average Oriceran."

Detective Lafayette finished clicking a few more options and shook his head. "Level four sounds good, but we still don't have a lot of information. What if they can't find him?"

"Doesn't matter." Detective West narrowed his eyes at the lines listing the victims. "Think about our guy's actions so far. Just because he's got some fancy powers doesn't change the fact that he's like a lot of regular serial killers."

"What do you mean?"

"He's power-tripping. Once he smells hunters coming, he'll go to them to make a point. Send the bounty request, and I bet you the bastard will all but run to the first bounty hunter."

***

Sample XJ422 stared down at the phone he'd taken from one of the victims. He'd been waiting for the police to trace the phone and come for him. Killing a few police to demonstrate his power would help them understand his threat, but he'd waited, and no one had come.

They don't know. And if they don't, I should call them.

It was time to test his true power. Time to show the police they were nothing before him.

He lifted the phone, then lowered it. No. It wasn't time, not yet. He needed to generate more fear; to make more angels cry first. The suffering on their faces buoyed his heart and filled the hungry void in his soul better than any simple kill.

I need a new name—one that inspires terror.

Sample XJ422 frowned as he tried to recall his original name. It'd long since vanished, smothered by memories of darkness and pain.

The thought didn't bother him much. Few normal names spread terror.

Maybe the police have given me a name. They spread fear even when they don't want to.

He raised the phone again and brought up the browser. A moment later he was at the Las Vegas Metropolitan Police Department official webpage. Flashing text on the side caught his attention.

NEW OFFICIAL LEVEL-FOUR BOUNTY ISSUED.

He tilted his head and tapped on the link.

A NEW LEVEL FOUR BOUNTY HAS BEEN ISSUED BY THE LAS VEGAS METROPOLITAN POLICE DEPARTMENT. IT HAS BEEN FUNDED BY THE CITY OF LAS VEGAS, CLARK COUNTY, AND A GENEROUS DONATION FROM THE NEVADA RESORT ASSO-CIATION.

Officially released information on "RED EYES Killer" as follows:

Unidentified killer, believed to be male, responsible for four homicides in the city of Las Vegas. Victims include three adult males and one adult female. Victim profiling suggests killer targets parents with young children. Killer isn't targeting children at this time but has previously demonstrated an inclination toward such potential murder targets.

Abilities include unidentified sensory manipulation manifesting as the ability to create localized darkness, resistance to small arms fire, and physical manipulation of own body to make weapons, included bone blades. Killer has previously demonstrated the ability to decapitate an adult male with such weapons.

A full physical description is not available at this time, but all witnesses report deepening shadows in the area and glowing red eyes.

Please be advised that this is classified as a LEVEL FOUR bounty at this time. Appropriate licensing is required for recovery of the bounty.

This is a LIVE recovery bounty. Termination of the bounty will result in forfeiture of fifty percent of the pre-tax value of the bounty.

All licensed bounty hunters attempting to capture the bounty should still exercise extreme caution and assume the bounty possesses additional weapons or abilities not specified in this bounty notice. Please note that these additional abilities may result in a more difficult bounty hunting experience than suggested by the current bounty level.

The city of Las Vegas and the Las Vegas Metropolitan Police Department are not responsible for any death, injury, or loss of property that occurs as a result of pursuing the Red-Eyes Killer.

Please be advised that any incidental damage or injury of third-parties will be the legal responsibility of the bounty hunter and not the city of Las Vegas or the Las Vegas Metropolitan Police Department.

Please note that all bounties are subject to the Nevada State Bounty Hunting Tax and Federal income taxes. Appropriate reporting forms will be sent to the IRS and Nevada Department of Taxation following award of the bounty.

Please click here for additional information, including further legal disclaimers.

"Level four? 'Red-Eyes Killer?' I think I prefer just 'Red Eyes.' They know fear now, but not enough." He crushed the phone in his hand and tossed the splintered mass of plastic and glass to the ground. "They need to recognize my true power. Soon they will know terror that will be spoken of for generations."

Red Eyes let out a low hollow laugh. Soon every angel in heaven would cry.

―――――

Doctor Simmons let out a long, pained sigh as he read the bounty report on the large projected screen at the front of the conference room. Four suited men turned to look at him.

"The sample isn't contained, Simmons," observed a

silver-haired man with a severe face. Doctor Anders. "Our…investors will be very displeased. This is an unmitigated disaster."

"Investors? You mean those damned gangsters? We should have never agreed to take their money."

Doctor Anders snorted. "You didn't seem to care about their background until a few days ago. All you cared about was their money, and if we recover the sample, we can continue to care only about their money."

"We can…still salvage this. It doesn't have to be a problem."

"How?"

Doctor Simmons pointed toward the screen. "Look at the notice. It's clear the police don't know much. They have only the most generic description. They can't trace it to us."

Doctor Anders slammed his hand on the table. "We were supposed to find the sample before the police. If the authorities get their hands on it they might be able to trace it back to our lab, especially if they get a wizard involved." He looked at each man in turn. "I think we can all agree, even setting aside our investors, that we don't want Oricerans realizing that we've been performing genetic engineering experiments involving mixing different types of Oriceran and pure human DNA. They'd destroy this lab if they realized what we could accomplish without using any magic as long as we have access to biological samples from magical beings."

"Just authorize the release of a team, and I'll make sure they recover the sample before the police or a bounty hunter. Then we won't have to worry about our investors or the Oricerans."

Doctor Anders nodded. "Very well. At this point, it doesn't matter if we recover the sample alive. Just make sure its corpse is back in this lab before anyone else finds it." He stood and adjusted his tie. "I'll contact our investors and make it clear that we're handling this matter."

Another member of management cleared his throat. "But what happens if the police or a bounty hunter captures the sample?"

"If that happens, you'd better hope your life insurance premiums are paid up."

9

James walked down the street, his hands in his pockets, only a quarter of a mile between him and a few In-N-Out Double-Doubles animal-style. His rumbling stomach kept his mind focused on his mission and not worrying about Trey, Shay, or Alison. He wasn't even sure why he was so hungry, given how much he had eaten at Jessie Rae's earlier in the day.

Two men across the street ducked into a liquor store. One reached into his jacket and pulled out something. A hint of silver gleamed under the harsh light of a street lamp; a gun, perhaps, or maybe just an elaborate lighter. With the man's back turned James couldn't be sure.

He grunted.

Not my problem. I'm not a cop, I'm a bounty hunter. I should just keep walking. Keep my life simple. I doubt two random street punks have a bounty on them.

James put one foot in front of the other and forced his gaze away from the liquor store. The Double-Doubles called to him, and taking down some random hoods in a liquor store would not only *not* be worth his time, but it'd also mean he'd be hungry for that much longer.

He made it another few feet before he stopped and rolled his eyes. An image of Alison flashed in his mind.

If he walked past and someone got hurt, he could only imagine what Alison would say. She would stare up at him with accusation on her face and openly wonder why her dad was willing to scare some random boys at her school, but not stop criminals threatening others with guns.

"Son of a bitch," James mumbled. He turned toward the liquor store. "I've got to hit the can anyway."

Andy wiped his nose on his sleeve and looked around. A couple inspected wine bottles in the back, and another man was wandering the beer aisle rubbing his chin like some sort of poor man's beer sommelier.

"Yo, Jake," he whispered. "I don't know, man. There are too many people here. This won't be clean. You said it'd be clean."

"Fuck that noise," the other hood whispered back. "Unless they got fucking machine guns hidden in their pockets, I give exactly zero fucks. We just need to hurry up and do this thing, bro."

The door chimed behind them, but they kept their attention on one another. One more customer wouldn't make a difference at that point.

"Maybe if we wait a few minutes some of these other people will leave," Andy suggested. He turned his head just in time to see the bathroom door close. "Fuck, did you see who came in?"

Jake shook his head. "No. Doesn't matter anyway." He snickered. "Unless it's some fucking cop."

"Fuck. Let's just do this shit."

James had just finished his business when the alarm rang.

He zipped up with a sigh. "At least they let me finish pissing first." He cracked his knuckles and opened the bathroom door. It was time to educate a couple of young men about situational awareness.

The two glaring hoods stood in front of the cashier waving their .22 revolvers around. A large glass barrier had descended from the ceiling, separating the cashier from the robbers.

"You better open that shit back up," one of the hoods shouted. He pointed his gun at the couple with fear and confusion on their faces holding wine bottles. "If you don't open up, I'll shoot one of these assholes. You willing to have that on your conscience, man?"

The other hood pointed his gun at a man cowering on his knees in the beer aisle. "And we'll cap this dude, too."

The cashier shook his head. "The police are already on their way. Just drop your guns and give up and it won't be a big deal. We both know that pieces of shit like you will be back on the street in months anyway. This doesn't have to be a big thing."

"You think I'm playing, bro?" the first hood yelled. He

fired at the cashier. Thin cracks spiderwebbed out from the point of impact, but the glass didn't break.

The woman screamed, and her husband covered her with his body. Their dropped wine bottles shattered on the floor, splattering wine all over their clothes.

The man in the beer aisle covered his head with his hands and sobbed quietly.

The hood punched the glass a few times. "Fuck this noise!" He ran to the front door and tried to open it, only to find it locked. You think I'm playing, bro? Seriously?" He spun on his heel and marched toward the couple.

The man lifted his fists, but the hood knocked him to the floor with a quick blow from the butt of his pistol. He pointed the gun right at the woman's head. She whimpered, and her eyes widened.

"I'm gonna count to ten, and if you don't open that glass or let us out, this bitch is dead." A muffled siren sounded in the distance. "Oh, sure, if it's not *my* ass robbing the local liquor store, the cops can't be found." He waved the gun around. "Why the fuck is this so hard tonight?"

James was done with this bullshit. The only thing more annoying than a criminal was an incompetent and whiny one. He stomped toward the man holding the gun on the woman.

The hood spun toward him. "You think you're gonna be a hero, you ugly son of a bi—"

The bounty hunter grabbed the man's wrist and yanked his arm upward. The gun discharged into the ceiling, showering both men with plaster and wood.

James pulled the hood forward and introduced his hard forehead to the other man's face, and blood spurted from the man's broken nose as he collapsed to the ground groaning. The bounty hunter tossed the gun to the ground and narrowed his eyes at the man's partner.

"Jake!" the other hood shouted, then to Brownstone, "You'll pay for that."

"Last chance to give up, asshole," James rumbled. "Keep going, and I'm gonna get seriously pissed. You interrupted my dinner."

A police car screeched to the stop in the parking lot.

The two officers waited, their guns pointed at the front window as they knelt behind their car. They jerked down as bullets shattered the glass.

Officer Silvers kept his back against the car and prepared to return fire. "Fuck. What the hell is going on in there?"

His partner gritted his teeth. "We need to move now. We can't wait for backup."

Two thuds followed, and the cops risked a peek, their guns ready. Two bodies lay on the ground, obviously thrown through the shattered window.

Officer Silvers blinked. "What the fuck?"

A moment later, a dark form climbed through the window. The cops pointed their weapons.

"Las Vegas PD!" the cops shouted in unison.

"Holy shit!" Officer Silvers appended a moment later. "That's James Brownstone!"

The cops' attention dropped to the bodies on the ground. Soft groans came from both men. Whoever they were, they were still alive, and the presence of the bounty hunter suggested they weren't the innocent victims in the situation.

The officers exchanged looks but kept their guns raised. James Brownstone was as famous for bringing on trouble as he was solving it, and this wasn't LA.

Brownstone finished his exit and brushed some glass off his jacket and pants. He stomped over to the two groaning men and yanked them up by the scruffs of their necks.

"Probably gonna try and sue me or some shit," the bounty hunter muttered. He dragged them over to the cops and tossed them on the ground. "Armed robbers. Got plenty of witnesses inside and surveillance video of them pistol-whipping a guy, shooting at someone, and generally being assholes."

The cops blinked and nodded.

Brownstone shrugged. "I've got shit to do."

Officer Silvers cleared his throat. "We're going to need an official statement, Mr. Brownstone."

"I just gave you one." He grunted and walked away. "I don't want to do paperwork. It messes up my feng shui or some shit like that. Plus, I'm hungry as fuck." He continued walking.

The second cop, Officer Riviera, turned to his partner. "What should we do? Stop him?"

"Do *you* want to try and stop James Brownstone?" Officer Silvers pointed to the downed criminals. "A guy who just did that? Let alone half the other stuff he's done? We'd need a whole AET team to stop James Brownstone."

"But what about procedure? And where the hell is he going?"

Officer Silvers spotted a familiar red, white, and yellow sign. "Don't worry. Let's get these guys in the cruiser and talk to the witnesses first. I think I know exactly where he's going."

They cuffed the suspects and shoved them in the back of their cruiser. Officer Silvers then headed into the now-open liquor store, shaking his head as he passed the destroyed window.

"I'm Officer Silvers," he announced as he entered the store. "Is everyone all right?"

The cashier pressed a button, and the glass partition slowly rose, accompanied by loud grinding. He pointed at a sniffling woman holding her husband. The man was conscious, but blood ran down the side of his head.

"Those maniacs were going to kill us all," the woman shouted. "If it wasn't for that large man I'd be dead!"

Officer Silvers nodded and headed over to the wounded man. "Sir, are you okay?"

The man looked up and winced. "I've felt better, but I'll live." He sat up. "The bastard just caught me by surprise, is all."

"Let me call an ambulance, and then I'll take all of your statements."

Thirty minutes later a police van had picked up the suspects, the witness statements had been taken, and the injured man was at the hospital with his wife. All in all, it had been a pretty clean operation for an armed robbery where actual gunfire and property destruction had taken place.

The evidence all seemed to point to that being the case because of James Brownstone's involvement. Every witness reported that the robbers had been about to execute the woman.

Officer Silvers was grateful no one had died, but that didn't change the reality that he still needed a few things from Brownstone.

He slid into his police cruiser and looked at his partner. "We've got everything pretty much taken care of, but there's one loose end."

"What?"

"James Brownstone. We don't have his statement."

His partner sighed. "Are we sure it's him?"

Officer Silvers snorted. "You know anyone else who looks like that who can do that sort of thing? He didn't deny it when we used his name, either."

"Do we need it? I mean, we got everyone else's statement."

"The captain's already chewed my ass twice this month for incomplete paperwork." Officer Silvers shook his head. "And yours, too, so we're going to have to decide who we're more afraid of—James Brownstone, or the captain."

"Captain hasn't personally wiped out any major gangs to my knowledge."

"Yeah, I agree."

"Still, I don't want to get my ass chewed." Officer Riviera looked out the window. "You said you know where Brownstone went?"

The other cop pointed into the distance. "Yeah, not exactly major detective work. There's an In-N-Out burger over there, and he mentioned being hungry. Let's go see if he's still there."

"What if he's not?"

"Then we'll figure something out."

Officers Silvers and Riviera stepped into the In-N-Out burger, half-hoping the famous bounty hunter had already finished his meal and taken off. Pissing off a man who could throw two criminals through a window with ease wasn't their idea of brave. It was just stupid.

Luck was a vengeful goddess that night. The wall of muscle sat at a table in the corner munching on a Double-Double, with the wrappers for a couple others wadded up in front of him.

Fuck, how much does this guy eat?

The police marched toward him. Both men's hearts pounded.

Officer Silvers took a deep breath and swallowed. "Mr. Brownstone? Um, may we have permission to talk with you?"

The bounty hunter looked up from the table. "Sure. What did you need?"

"We…um… We kind of…need your statement."

The cop's heart thundered as he waited for the bounty hunter to pick him up and toss him through a window.

"Do I have to write anything?" Brownstone inquired.

Both cops shook their head.

Brownstone gestured toward the chairs across the table. "Then I'm more than happy to help. Sorry about walking off before, but I was just so damned hungry." He munched on his Double-Double. "Ask me whatever." He nodded toward the front. "You might want to grab some food first if it's gonna be a while. I forgot how good these were. It's not Jessie Rae's, but it's still a fine meal."

Officer Silvers let out a nervous chuckle. "Uh, that's okay. We'll just get the statement."

10

Trey took a deep breath as he pulled the truck into the lot outside of the park. Even though he'd agreed to meet his aunt, he wanted to make sure it was somewhere she couldn't immediately ask for money or easily ambush him, and a wide-open park was good a choice as any. Suspicion from both his time as a gang leader and his more recent time as bounty hunter refused to let his heart settle.

Never trust what someone tells you when they're desperate. People lie even when they aren't *desperate.*

A small spark of hope tried to push through the distrust and allow him to believe that the woman wanted something other than money. The spark flared into something brighter—the promise of new family.

Don't get conned. This might not be anything. Her call was just as convenient as all the ones from all the other people suddenly interested in reconnecting with me.

Trey stepped out of his F-350 and started up a sidewalk leading to a small playground in the distance. The morning sun still hung low in the cloudless sky as he closed on the area. A woman in a faded blue dress sat on a bench. His heart skipped a beat.

Keep it cool. This could still be a trick. It might not even be Auntie Charlyce.

He continued up the path and closed on the bench. The woman turned to face him.

Trey sucked in a breath and his heart thundered. Seven years was a long time. It'd added lines to her face, and the hard living had probably added a few dozen more, but there was no doubt the woman sitting on the bench was his Aunt Charlyce.

He swallowed and approached the bench with his hands in the pockets of his suit jacket. Verifying it was her didn't change anything in his brain, but his heart didn't want to listen.

"Hey," Trey offered. He chuckled. "Long time, no see."

Charlyce stood, trembling slightly. "I've been scared, Trey. All this time, but especially when you agreed to come. I'm not the woman you knew before, and I'm ashamed of that. It means a lot that you came, because I know you didn't have to."

Tears welled up in Trey's eyes. Seven years. With his mother long gone, he'd only had his nana as far as close relatives went. Now a family member stood right in front of him, one he'd thought was long dead. It was like being given a gift he hadn't even known he wanted.

The dam inside him broke, and he rushed forward to envelop the woman in a big, loving crush. Charlyce let out a yelp of surprise as Trey hugged her, saying nothing else for a good thirty seconds before breaking into sobs.

"I'm so sorry, Trey. I'm so sorry. I screwed up."

Trey swallowed and pulled away from his aunt. He grabbed a handkerchief from his pocket to hand to her and dried his eyes on his sleeve.

"It don't matter now," he offered, his voice quivering. "I've screwed up a lot in my life, so I ain't about to look down my nose at you. Someone offered me a hand up and he wasn't even my family, so how can I not offer *you* a hand up?" He shook his head. "No family of mine is going to be living on the street when I can give them a room."

"Bless you, boy. Bless you." Charlyce dabbed at her eyes with the handkerchief. "I'm so sorry."

Trey managed a smile. Bittersweet tears threatened to return, but he held them back. Not out of shame or pride— finding a lost loved one was more than enough reason to cry, but he didn't want to make his aunt anymore upset than she was.

"Like I told you the other day," Trey managed to get out, "Nana told me you had disappeared. I knew you drank a little bit too much, so I just always figured it was that."

Charlyce sighed. "It started that way, but the problem was a boyfriend I was dating at the time. He convinced me of a lot of lies, like that he'd amount to something and that I should go with him. He's the one who introduced me to heroin."

Trey winced. "Damn." His face tightened. "This guy still around? I'd like to have a conversation with him." His hands tightened into fists.

His aunt shrugged. "Maybe. I don't know. Lost contact with him years ago, but it doesn't matter. One thing I've learned is that I have to forgive others. He might be the one who introduced me to drugs, but I'm the one who kept taking them." She sighed. "The years passed in a haze until eighteen months ago when I realized I needed to stop or I'd end up dead or with some disease. It took me a while to fight it, but now I'm clean. Been trying to save and looking into a job, but I know it's gonna take a while. Not like people are eager to hire ex-addicts who still live on the street."

Trey placed his hand on his shoulder. "Like I said, you're coming back to LA with me. I know Nana will be happy to see you. Even though she told me you disappeared, I always knew she was sad and wanted to see you again."

"You really think so?"

He nodded. "I *know* so. It'll be good for us to be together again. We're family, and that means something."

"But I failed her. I failed you. I failed everyone."

Trey snorted. "Because you did some things you ain't proud of? I bet you'd need to be on the streets for another seven years to catch up to me when it comes to that. It don't matter. Family is family, and we're gonna make sure you get back on your feet. I've got a good honest job now, where I help protect people. So I'm gonna help protect my auntie."

Charlyce let out a contented sigh and smiled. She gestured toward his suit. "Look at you, big-time fancy bounty hunter on television. I always worried..." She shook her head. "It don't matter now, I guess."

"You're right. I'm a bounty hunter now, and on the right side of the law. You might have been on the streets and taking drugs, but now you're off drugs and soon you'll be off the street. I know first-hand how when you give someone a chance they can turn into something better than they ever thought." He took a few deep breaths and smiled.

Trey's aunt pulled him in for another tight hug. They stayed that way for a long moment before separating.

Charlyce looked him in the eyes and nodded. "The person who gave you a chance—it's him, right? James Brownstone?"

Trey gave her a quick nod. "Yeah."

"I need to get in contact with him. Not about money, but about that demon I was telling you about."

He held up a hand. "I can get a hold of my boss, but not before I get some food into you." He gestured toward his truck. "Follow me."

Charlyce fell in behind Trey as he headed toward the truck. When her head ducked for a moment, he sent a quick text to the big man.

I need a favor. Please call me when you get a chance.

The phone chimed only a few seconds later.

I can do you one better. Send me your address, and I can be there in half an hour.

Trey stared at his phone and looked back at his aunt. "There a place to eat nearby?"

"There's a Denny's down the block."

"We'll hit that then."

He grabbed the address from a map app and texted it to James.

I'll be there with my aunt, and she needs your help.

The big man is in Vegas? I bet he came for that barbeque again.

Trey chuckled and shook his head. He didn't care if it was divine providence, luck, or just the natural consequence of a barbeque obsession, but having James close by filled him with confidence. Even if the big man couldn't help his aunt with her request, he'd already led her to Trey.

James Brownstone had not only pulled Trey away from a life of crime, but he'd also indirectly helped reunite his family.

Damn, James. Pace yourself!

Three suited men stepped into the dark abandoned warehouse, assault rifles at the ready. Sunlight streamed through the windows, cutting through the shadows and highlighting the thick clouds of dust floating in the air. Crates, stray bits of plastic, and broken mannequins covered the floor.

A dead building. The perfect place for a freak mutant to hide.

"Is this the right place?" one of the men asked.

The team leader nodded. "Yeah, Doctor Simmons said the sample would be within a few hundred feet of this location, based on what the satellite data said. Something about an energy signature. I don't know the details. It's all science shit. We'll just have to find him in here."

The third team member shook his head. "Stupid freak. It should have just stayed in the lab."

"Should I have now?" interjected a hollow voice from a corner.

The three men spun, aiming their rifles. Glowing red eyes peered out of the darkness.

"Sample XJ422," shouted the team leader. "We have orders to recover you for the lab, dead or alive. If you surrender immediately, we won't gun your ass down."

Laughter echoed in the cavernous space of the warehouse. "I am no longer Sample XJ422. I am Red Eyes. I am Death. I am Terror."

"This is your last chance to surrender, freak."

"You said too much before. Energy signature? This was their only chance of finding me. Once I kill you, I know what I have to do to hide."

The shadows spread from the corner and the figure burst into a sprint.

"Light him up!" the team leader shouted.

Burst-fired bullets peppered the walls as the men tried to bring down their enemy. The shadows stopped spreading, and XJ422 leapt to the other side of the room, revealing his leathery and mottled naked body. A bullet struck him, and he hissed in pain.

The shadows cloaking the corners of the room vanished. It'd be a stretch to call the warehouse well-lit, but it was noticeably brighter than before.

Yeah. You're not so tough, you freaky piece of shit.

The team leader grinned and fired another burst. He narrowly missed as the mutant jumped behind some crates. A trail of blood spots led right to his hiding place.

"That's right, fucker. We're not some idiot tourist with a tiny little pop gun. You should have surrendered, XJ422. At least the lab would have kept your sorry ass alive for a little while longer."

The team leader reloaded and gestured to the two other men to advance. Disappointment stabbed his gut. He'd always wondered what it'd be like to take on one of the stronger mutants from the lab. Most he'd seen were useless freaks that couldn't last more than a few days, but a few like XJ422 looked like more fun. What a damned waste.

"Come out, come out, wherever you are," the team leader sang. "I'm feeling nice. Come out with your hands up, and you still get to live…at least until you get back to the lab."

A crate flew toward the team leader and he opened fire. The bullets ripped into the wood but didn't do much to alter its course. The box slammed into him, and he fell with a grunt.

XJ422 leapt toward one of the team members, one of his arms now tipped with a bone blade and the other contorting into a barbed tentacle.

The unlucky team member managed to get off a single shot before the mutant cleaved his arm at the shoulder. The man screamed as he fell to the ground, blood gushing everywhere. The mutant finished him by ripping his heart out with the tentacle and tossing it to the ground.

"Fuck!" The team leader flipped his rifle to automatic and held down the trigger.

The sample jerked a few times, then yanked his dead team member up. Bullets ripped through the corpse, but a second later the team leader realized that XJ422 didn't want the man's body as a shield. The tentacle twisted and deformed into a leathery arm, and the sample threw the corpse toward the remaining members of the recovery team. The two men ducked out of the way.

The team leader brought up his rifle and squeezed the trigger again. The weapon clicked. Empty.

"Shit." He backpedaled and ejected the magazine, reaching into his pocket for a second.

Blood coated the sample, both from its victim and several oozing bullet wounds. The team leader smiled as he slapped in the new magazine. They were winning. Mutant bullshit wasn't a match for a good old-fashioned automatic weapon.

The smugness disappeared a few seconds later when XJ422 slashed open the neck of his remaining team member with a bone blade. There wasn't a clear separation of head and body. Blood sprayed from the dying man's neck, and his head flopped. He collapsed to the ground.

"You son of a bitch!"

The team leader held down the trigger again, spewing 5.56 bullets toward his bleeding enemy. He wasn't going to die in an abandoned warehouse at the hands of some lab freak.

The sample jerked with each bullet, and its blood painted the ground. It collapsed to its knees and then onto its chest.

The team leader took several deep breaths. He'd done it. He'd killed the fucker.

He advanced on the corpse, grinning. He felt a little pity for the other men, but it wasn't like he knew them well, and any battle he walked away from was a win.

"Should have taken my offer to go back to the lab, freak."

The sample jumped up, and pain blasted through the man's arm. He tried to pull his trigger, only to realize an agonizing few seconds later that his right forearm was missing and his gun was on the ground with his arm.

The humanoid creature in front of him licked his blood off the bone blade, then sliced his other arm off. The team leader fell to the ground screaming in pain.

XJ422 leaned over him, his red eyes glowing brighter than before. His wounds started to close.

"I listened in the lab, even when they thought I wasn't. I know things they don't think I know." He knelt by the dying man and grinned, revealing a mouth filled with sharp fangs. "Plenty of animals eat, but they aren't like me. They can't assimilate DNA. None of the sheep before were worth it, but you've proven yourself worthy to become one with Death." He licked his lips. "And you've brought me wonderful toys, too. I appreciate you providing me with support like this."

The team leader screamed as XJ422's fangs ripped into his throat.

11

Maria stepped into the Black Sun. She didn't usually hit the bar in the morning, so the lack of a crowd took her by surprise. It'd been a while since she'd seen the place so empty.

Guess even criminals don't drink before lunch.

The AET lieutenant sidled up to the bar. She gave Kathy a polite nod, but she wasn't interested in a drink. She needed Tyler. "Your boss around?"

Kathy nodded. "He's in the back."

"Could you get him for me?"

Kathy smiled. "Sure thing, Lieutenant." The brunette made her way from the bar to a back hallway, and a moment later she reappeared with Tyler in tow.

Tyler chuckled. "Don't usually see you here in the morning, Lieutenant. What's the occasion?"

Maria shrugged. "I'm not here for booze."

Tyler went behind the bar and leaned forward. "What do you need then, Lieutenant?"

"I've got some information suggesting a level-five

bounty might be coming into town, and I wondered if you'd heard anything."

The bartender sighed and rubbed the back of his neck. "I'm sorry, but I can't help you, Lieutenant. Not for a level five."

Maria blinked. "Huh?"

He held up his hands. "Look, I've got a policy. Small fish are small fish. If they are level three or lower we can talk about information, but a man or a woman who has earned a level four or higher bounty... Well, I don't want to be on their bad side."

She glowered at him. "What about being on *my* bad side?"

Tyler shrugged. "At least a cop won't melt my skin or turn me into a zombie." He looked around for a moment before lowering his voice. "I can't give you anything else, but I will let you know that, yes, a level five just came to LA."

Maria locked eyes with the bartender. She could threaten or arrest him, but if she did that all the careful neutrality they'd worked to build at the Black Sun would vanish. Even if they had to look the other way now and again, overall, having access to the place worked to the cops' advantage.

She sucked in a breath and nodded. "Not going to say I'm happy about it, but I understand." She shrugged. "I've got another question that shouldn't offend your delicate criminal sensibilities."

Tyler chuckled. "What?"

"Even though the Oricerans coughed up a bunch of money to donate to the police department and AET, replacing a lot of the equipment and artifacts we used recently is hard and it's going to take a while through normal channels."

"Oh?"

"Yeah, you think government requisitions are a bureaucratic nightmare? Try doing it for magical items. It has to go through so many damn departments and approvals." Maria shook her head. "It's like everyone's afraid we'll accidentally give a necromancer taxpayer dollars and someone will vote out the city council and the mayor because of it."

"So you're looking for what…unofficial channels?"

Maria shrugged. "Just want to know all my options."

"You have any contacts with the consulate?"

She shook her head. "No. I don't, but that's a good idea."

"Yeah, well, they'll try and keep it official, and they are pretty bureaucratic, too. But if you're looking for something a little less official, I can give you a name."

"Go on."

"Dannec. He's an elf." Tyler grinned. "But I wouldn't go talking to him dressed for the office, if you know what I mean." He rattled off an address. "Are you sure about this, Lieutenant? Blurring some lines here."

A fucking level five is in town, and we barely have any anti-magic deflectors. It's a damned slaughter waiting to happen.

Maria snorted. "Even though we have the money, the bureaucrats are dragging their feet on replacement equipment. My men need the gear to survive, and if I need to bend the rules a little to do it, I don't give a shit. Thanks, Tyler." She hopped off her stool and marched toward the door.

James slid into the booth next to Trey and across from his aunt. He could see the family resemblance, and made sure not to comment on her lean appearance and the sunken cheeks that indicated malnourishment.

"It's a pleasure to meet you, Mr. Brownstone," the woman offered. "I'm Charlyce."

"Nice to meet you, Charlyce. Didn't know Trey had an aunt."

Trey sighed, but the woman smiled.

"I've been on the streets, but I've cleaned myself up. We haven't seen each other for seven years."

"Shit, seven years?" He glanced at Trey, and the man shrugged.

Charlyce waved a hand. "But that can wait for another time. I'm not here to talk about me, but a little girl named Dina."

James leaned back in the booth. "Who's that?"

"Her daddy was killed right in front of her. I found her hiding in a vent in an alley."

The bounty hunter shot another glance at Trey before looking back at Charlyce. "That's terrible, but what does it have to do with me?"

"They're not talking a lot about it, but something evil done killed that girl's father." Charlyce shook her head. "It cut his head off. I overheard the police at the scene when they were talking to the girl. She talked about weird shadows and glowing red eyes, and when I found her, she told me 'Red Eyes' had killed her daddy." The woman reached across the table and took James' hand. "Please, Mr.

Brownstone. This is something evil and magical. I saw the body. No normal man could do what I saw. Las Vegas needs you. Dina needs you."

James' face twitched. "What's this girl to you?"

"Nothing, really, I guess... I'll admit I've been trying to keep an eye on her. She lost her daddy, you know? Since her daddy's murder they've been keeping her at a Child Protective Services building, but I don't know if I trust them. The girl ain't got no family, so I want to do what I can to help her and get some justice for her." She clucked her tongue. "She ain't the only one. Been several deaths lately. The police are keeping a lot of details out of the news, but I've heard some of them when they didn't know I was around and listening."

James frowned and turned to Trey. "Have you checked the local bounties?"

The other man shrugged. "I just came here for her."

"And I just came for Jessie Rae's." James pulled out his phone and brought up his bounty hunting app. He tapped to change the location from Los Angeles to Las Vegas and searched for new bounties. "We got a new one recently. Level four, 'Red Eyes Killer.' Looking through the shit they have listed, this sounds like the guy."

Charlyce nodded grimly. "Will you help, Mr. Brownstone?"

James grunted. "I was looking for something to do anyway."

"Bless you, Mr. Brownstone. Bless you."

Trey furrowed his brow. "I want in on this, James."

The bounty hunter looked at his protégé. Trey had done a good job proving himself in Los Angeles, but a level four with unusual powers might prove too dangerous. Telling him that directly might wound his pride, though.

Time to make my life more complicated by lying. Shit. Hope this doesn't become a habit.

"You need to stay with your aunt. First of all, you should catch up with her since you haven't seen her for years. Plus, if she's keeping an eye on the girl, you can help with that just in case the guy pokes around the girl again."

James doubted the killer would, but at least this way Trey could feel involved.

Trey nodded. "You got it, big man."

Charlyce smiled. "Thank you for taking the time to listen to a homeless nobody, Mr. Brownstone."

"You aren't homeless anymore," her nephew interjected. "You were *never* homeless. You were just lost."

Maria stepped out of her car and scanned the area. Dilapidated apartment buildings lined the street, and more than a few rough-looking men, some wearing gang colors, prowled around. That wasn't that different than many other places in LA. The pointed-eared man staring at her from across the street was more what she was looking for.

Even though most people called the area Elf Town, plenty of different Oricerans lived in the neighborhood, both new arrivals and Earth families with Oriceran blood. Some had known and hidden their true nature throughout the generations, and others had only recently learned of their heritage. The neighborhood wasn't the only

Oriceran-heavy enclave in the city, but this was where Dannec lived.

Maria tugged at her black jacket, not liking the idea that she was doing something for the police out of uniform. Her blue jeans, black leather boots, white shirt, and black jacket wouldn't stand out here, but neither did they command the respect associated with a police uniform.

The AET lieutenant made her way down the street as she watched the building numbers go up. She was almost to her contact's apartment.

"Yo, baby," a man called from across the street. "I got something you'd like."

Maria flipped him off and continued walking. The man chuckled.

Another man grabbed his crotch. "Welcome to the neighborhood, sweet thing."

She snorted.

A lot of people misunderstood both Maria and AET. She didn't give two shits if someone was a man or an elf or a half-dragon or whatever, let alone if they had been born on Oriceran or Earth. America was a land of immigrants, and if some of the new ones came from another planet, that wasn't a reason to hate them. People were people.

She only had a problem with criminals and overpowered beings who thought they were above the law. The average Oriceran in town kept their nose clean and followed the law while plenty of humans like Brownstone caused trouble.

Things might change in the future, but for now the powerful needed to be kept in check, and AET was a big part of that.

Maria stopped when she spotted a blue apartment building with the correct street number. She marched up the rickety, rusted staircase to the second floor and then to an apartment in the back, then took a deep breath and knocked on the faded door. The metal numbers marking the apartment were gone; only their outline remained.

The lock turned, and the door partially opened. The top chain remained in place. A frail ancient-looking elf peered at Maria through the crack of the door.

He looked her up and down. "I don't know you. Who are you?"

"Maria."

"What do you want?"

"I'm looking for Dannec." She leaned closer to whisper. "To talk about buying a few magical items."

"I don't know about that kind of thing."

Maria laughed. "You're an elf who doesn't know about magic? Bullshit."

"It's a strange new world, isn't it? Lots of strange people in it."

"Look, Tyler at the Black Sun told me to talk to you."

The elf narrowed his eyes. "Did he now?"

"Yeah."

The door closed.

"Shit." Maria gritted her teeth. She'd fucked it up already.

A moment later it swung open, now chain-free, and the elf gestured. "Come on in."

Maria stepped inside and held in the gasp that wanted to erupt. Piles of magical items and artifacts sat atop several tables in the living room. Rods, wands, crystals, necklaces, bones, coins, and an assortment of other miscellaneous objects covered the tables.

Her instincts as a cop told her that half the shit in that room was probably illegal, but she wasn't there to put the man in jail. She was there to get what she needed to protect her AET team. Besides, there was a difference between feeling something might be illegal and *knowing* it was illegal.

The elf looked her up and down again, suspicion in his eyes. "And what are you interested in, Maria?"

She slowly reached into her pocket and pulled out a discharged anti-magic deflector. The crystal was solid black.

Dannec held out his hand and Maria placed the deflector in his palm.

"Good stuff," the elf murmured. "Not just *good* stuff, government stuff." He peered at her. "This is specially made, Maria. I don't think this is something a random woman off the street can get."

"I didn't say I was a random woman."

"If you want me to help you, be honest with me. It's only fair, don't you think?"

Maria glanced at the door and considered leaving before shaking her head. "It's AET issue. I work with AET. Lieutenant Maria Hall, LAPD."

The elf's bored expression didn't change. "And why is AET interested in old Dannec, huh? You think I'm an enhanced threat?" He chuckled. "My wife would agree."

"We're not, not officially. I'm interested in you getting me more deflectors, or something that works the same. I don't care." Maria shrugged. "My men need protection, and the word is you can get them that."

"I can, for a price."

"I can get you money."

Dannec gave her a toothy grin. "That I like to hear. I read about it, you know."

"Read about what?"

The elf waved a hand in a grand gesture. "The big battle. I've heard rumors and whispers about it as well." He shook his head. "You're lucky to be alive, Lieutenant."

Maria snorted and pointed at the deflector. "It wasn't luck. It was equipment, and that's what I need from you."

Dannec nodded. "Of course." He handed the spent deflector back. "You know what you should have done in that last battle?"

"What?"

"You should have called James Brownstone to help. You know, the one who the police had kill all the gangsters."

Maria managed a pained smile. "We do often go after the same targets, true, but this wasn't a matter where Brownstone could help the department."

She saw no reason for this elf to know about her feelings about Brownstone.

"I see. I also read about how many deflectors you used up in the battle," Dannec commented. "You want that many from me?"

Maria nodded. "Yes."

He rattled off a high price, and the cop twitched. She hadn't expected them to be cheap, but the shock of hearing the amount still took her by surprise.

Dannec clucked his tongue. "Don't worry, Lieutenant

Hall. These are better, probably thirty percent more absorption, than your fancy government-issued ones." He rubbed his chin. "Because I like your face, I will take fifteen percent off the price, but you'll have to owe me a favor."

Maria narrowed her eyes. "A favor?"

"Yes, a favor." He shrugged. "Nothing illegal. Just a favor."

Maria gritted her teeth and again considered walking out. Even if the favor weren't illegal, owing a man with criminal connections was dangerous. But then she remembered the battle in the park: wounded men on the ground, the damned witch repelling bullets like it was nothing.

"Fair enough," she muttered.

"Good, good. One last thing."

"Yeah?"

Dannec grinned. "Magic takes many forms. Do you or your men have any restrictions?"

"Restrictions?"

"You know, like refusing to wear chicken bones or skulls?"

Maria grimaced at the idea of the AET walking around holding skulls or wearing chicken bones. "Uh…"

Dannec cackled.

She blinked. "You're fucking with me, aren't you?"

"Yes, but you should have seen your face."

Maria cracked a smile. "You're all right, Dannec."

T essa strolled down the street, taking in the Hollywood Walk of Fame with its speckled terrazzo blocks with five-pointed stars set inside. She passed name after name, but she couldn't bring herself to care. Tourists strolled on either side of her, taking pictures or seeking the star of their favorite entertainer. More than a few people clapped with excitement when they finally located the star they were looking for.

The woman snorted, drawing a few curious looks from passing tourists. The actors, directors, and musicians who had earned themselves a spot on the Walk of Fame had accomplished that through mere entertainment efforts, and entertainment was a lie. Even worse, it was a distraction from the truth of human existence.

The true human experience was distilled pain and misery. Enlightenment and kindness were a lie. Only strength and power freed you from the darkness.

Tessa shook her head. There were so many people around her, all with vacant and shallow expressions. In a sense, they weren't really people. They didn't have the strength to be worthy of the title "human." They were ghosts; pale reflections of living souls. They were dead but didn't know it.

I've proven myself strong. This is why I'm happy, and others are miserable in their hearts. It's why they seek to distract themselves with frivolousness.

Her hand dipped into her purse, and she caressed the emerald-tipped wand inside.

She stopped and watched the flow of foot traffic for a long moment. It'd be so easy to unleash her power and kill dozens if not hundreds of people. *Then* they would know misery and suffering. She'd prove her humanity over these ghosts calling themselves people.

The woman let out a long sigh. She wasn't worried about the police, even the AET. From what she'd heard, the main LA AET team had been hit hard by a strong witch the week before. Tessa doubted they had the resources to handle her. She licked her lips. It was tempting.

Tessa pulled her hand out of her purse.

No. The authorities were no threat, but one man was— a man who'd proven his humanity through the destruction of so many ghosts. James Brownstone.

"I'll be nice, Brownstone," Tessa whispered. "For now."

James pushed into the busy Las Vegas police station. A din of police, civilians, and bitching criminals filled the room. A few people glanced his way and whispered to themselves, but he didn't know if that was a good thing or a bad one.

He grunted. The bounty hunter was used to LA and LA cops, people like Sergeant Mack and his station. Even though James had been to Las Vegas many times, he'd barely dealt with the police and didn't know where the cops working their bounty department were located.

Sometimes a man just wanted some barbeque without trouble.

A detective in an ill-fitting suit looked his way and frowned.

Shit. They got a problem with me here? This might have been a bad idea.

The detective marched straight toward James, even pushing a handcuffed suspect out of the way.

"Watch it, bro!" the suspect shouted.

The cop flipped him off and continued on his path to James. He stopped right in front of the bounty hunter, looking him up and down.

"You're James Brownstone, right?"

"Yeah," James rumbled.

"Come with me." The detective spun on his heel and marched toward the front door.

The bounty hunter blinked a few times and shook his head. He had no idea why the cop would be leaving the building instead of taking him to another room inside. Maybe this was his way of telling James to get the hell out of Las Vegas, or something worse.

Fuck. Is this some sort of trap? Maybe they've got AET set up?

James walked after the detective, his muscles tensing.

He wanted to trust the police since they were on the same side, but his experiences with Lieutenant Hall and the AET in LA had made it all too clear that not every cop trusted him.

Still, what choice did he have? He needed the local cops to be on his side, and refusing to go with a detective because he was paranoid about an ambush wouldn't help with that.

The cop continued to the street and waited for the walk sign to change. He hurried across and James followed, now more confused than ever.

"I hear you like barbeque, Brownstone," the cop mentioned.

James chuckled. "Yeah, I like barbeque. I guess you could say I *really* like it. Didn't realize that was something people knew about me."

"Yeah, I love me some good barbeque myself." The cop shook his head. "Except for gas. It's just…"

"No bark," James finished for him.

"Yeah, exactly. Just not the flavor I want." The cop looked thoughtful for a moment. "If you love barbeque, there's one place you need to go. The best I've ever had, and I've had barbeque all over."

James waited, his heart rate kicking up at the possibility of discovering a place he'd somehow missed.

"It's called Jessie Rae's," the cop continued. "It's not a fancy place, so some people just pass it by, but it's damned barbeque perfection, I'm telling you. Won all sorts of awards."

James laughed. "Yeah, I know Jessie Rae's. I came here this trip to go there."

"You came to Vegas just for Jessie Rae's?"

"Yeah."

The cop scratched his chin. "You know what? Can't say I blame you. You're a man of discriminating taste, Brownstone."

James shrugged. "Not to be a dick, but where are we going?"

"Yeah, I guess I should have mentioned that to begin with. We're close to a CPS office. There's something I wanted to show you. I'm Detective West, by the way. I'm in homicide."

James remembered the name from the news report and some of the additional notes attached to the bounty. "You're one of the main guys investigating the Red Eyes Killer."

"Yeah, I am. We'll talk a little bit more about it after I show you something. I just want you to have all the important information before we start chatting."

The worn brick façade of the CPS building came into view about a block away. James' tension had vanished with the brief discussion of barbeque, but realizing the cop was attached to the bounty summoned it all back. He'd gone to the police station to talk to someone about the killer.

He might have come to Vegas for barbeque, but he was staying to take down a serial killer.

They arrived at the concrete steps leading to the front door of the CPS building. Once inside Detective West waved to a woman at the front desk, and she nodded toward a nearby hallway.

The cop didn't even slow as he turned into it. He led James to a room halfway down the corridor past an intersection and opened the door. The bounty hunter stepped inside. A one-way mirror dominated the center of the room.

Two young girls were playing with dolls in a small play-room on the other side of the mirror. A middle-aged woman in professional dress sat in a small chair looking at her phone. One of the children, a little blond girl, looked young—maybe four or five. The other was a few years older. James wasn't sure. He wasn't that good at guessing kids' ages.

Detective West cleared his throat. "Since you knew who I was, I'm guessing you were at the station to ask about the Red Eyes Killer."

James grunted. "Was gonna check into him, at least."

"Three little girls have lost their parents. One was lucky; she had relatives in town. These two have no close relatives, so we're going to have to put them into the system. That's what this asshole is doing, Brownstone. Butchering people, and not just killing them, killing them in front of their children." Detective West shook his head. "Even if these kids get into a stable new family situation, they're going to have to deal with having witnessed those murders for the rest of their lives. Think about how fucked up that is."

The little blond girl turned. It was as if she was looking right at James with her mournful gaze.

Orphans. Just like me.

His stomach knotted. What sort of horrible shit had he seen before his parents had sent him to Earth? He didn't remember those early years, but maybe that was a mercy.

James spun and stomped out of the room.

"Brownstone!" the cop called after him.

He ignored Detective West and walked around the corner toward the entrance to the playroom.

James threw open the door and marched right into the room. The woman in the chair let out a yelp and hopped up, almost dropping her phone.

"What are you doing, Brownstone?" Detective West inquired.

James stared down at the little girl. The other girl in the room gave him a quick glance before returning her attention to her doll.

The blond little girl stood. Her eyes widened. She took tiny steps until she stood right in front of him and wrapped her arms around his leg. Tears streamed down her face.

"I'm James Brownstone," he rumbled.

"I'm Dina." She sniffled. "I told Red Eyes that I'd get someone to punish them, and I asked the nice lady about finding you."

"Finding me?"

He glanced at the woman and she shrugged, confusion written all over her face.

The girl bobbed her head. "I prayed, and I asked the angels to bring you so you could find my daddy's killer and punish him. The old man on tv said you stop bad people."

Old man on tv? James stared down at the girl, a bit lost but understanding the most important thing: this little girl was suffering.

He picked the girl up. "Yeah, I stop bad people. No one hurts little girls. I'll take care of your daddy's killer."

The professional woman had put her phone away and

stepped forward with her arms out. James slipped the girl into the woman's arms with a sigh.

Detective West nodded toward the door. "We shouldn't be here, Brownstone."

James nodded and followed the cop outside.

The cop blew out a long breath. "Just to be clear, this isn't a dead or alive bounty, Brownstone. You take him out, you might lose fifty percent of the bounty, if not the whole thing."

"Sometimes it's not about the money." James glanced toward the door. "Sometimes it's about making sure little angels don't cry themselves to sleep at night fearing what is out there."

Trey's phone chimed for the fifteenth time in a half hour, and he groaned and shook his head.

"What do you think of this one, Trey?" Aunt Charlyce called from farther up the row of dresses. She held up an orange maxi.

Trey had insisted they go shopping. He of all people understood how new clothes could change a person's perspective and attitude.

"It looks good." He shrugged, and his phone chimed again.

All the messages were variations on the same, his boys bitching about Staff Sergeant Royce going all drill instructor on their asses. They needed to stop whining and start doing what their trainer told them. They weren't gangbangers anymore, and the minute they accepted that, the easier it'd be for them to transition to being bounty hunters.

His aunt draped another dress over her arm. "What's all those messages?"

"Complaints from my boys."

"You're a busy man. Shouldn't Mr. Brownstone be handling that sort of thing?"

Trey shook his head. "No. The big man needs to concentrate on the big threats. My boys and me, we're cleaning up the normal threats rather than the freaks, but I'm the one who led these boys, so it's my responsibility to make sure they get with the program." He chuckled. "We've got a Marine Corps drill instructor working with them. Some of my boys thought they knew tough, but between Mr. Brownstone and Staff Sergeant Royce they're learning what real toughness is."

Aunt Charlyce nodded. "It's good, what you're doing. What he's doing, too."

"I've always tried to give respect to get respect. The big man understands that so we've gotten along, but he's only one man, and he can only do so much. The Brownstone Agency is the next step." He shook his head. "Maybe the cops aren't as bad as I thought, but we both know they got their priorities. Maybe the Brownstone Agency will get so large we won't even need cops anymore."

"That'd be a sight." Her smile lit her face.

Trey furrowed his brow. "When was the last time you stayed somewhere nice, Auntie? Real nice?"

"It's not so bad now that I'm clean. The shelters have lots of rules against junkies, so I've had more warm beds lately."

Trey snorted. "I ain't talking about that. This is a family reunion, and I've got money now. I want to make sure you experience some nice stuff for a change."

"Nice stuff?" The woman stared at him, a puzzled expression taking over her face.

He grinned. "I've got just the idea." He whipped out his phone to text James.

Hey, big man. I went shopping with my aunt, and we're gonna go stay at the Aria tonight.

Trey couldn't think of anything nicer than a four-million-square-foot luxury resort.

Trey chuckled as he sat down at the fancy white wooden table near the doors to the balcony. His nana's whole house could almost fit inside the suite.

He tapped away at the app on his phone, looking for level one to three bounties. If he was going to stay in Las Vegas for a few days anyway, it might not hurt to pick up a little extra cash. His little trip to the Aria was going to blow through a lot of the cash he'd earned lately.

Not that he regretted it. He was happy to do something nice for his aunt, but he'd be even happier if his account grew instead of shrank.

Aunt Charlyce emerged from the bathroom. After their shopping trip and a visit to a hairdresser, she didn't look like a woman who'd spent seven years on the street. She just looked like some professional woman who needed to eat a little more.

"You're so hardworking, Trey."

He shrugged and scrolled through the potential bounties. "I thought the gang was my shot before, but this is my real shot. Mr. Brownstone's made it easy for me."

"I still don't understand how this all works. I saw you on the news so I get that you're going after people, but how is he involved?"

"It's his agency, but me, and soon a lot of the other boys, are his employees. We get the advantage of his rep, and we concentrate on all the bastards without freak powers since we can handle them. He gets a small cut."

His aunt frowned. "So he's making you risk everything and still taking money? He seemed like a good man, but now I don't know."

Trey burst out laughing. "Me risk everything?"

"What's so funny?"

"Have you *seen* some of the guys Mr. Brownstone has gone after?" He shook his head. "He's taken down guys who would have wiped out every last one of my boys and me even if we went after them together." Trey snorted. "Mr. Brownstone doesn't need to do any of this sh—"

He sighed. It wasn't like his homeless aunt hadn't lived around people with rough speech, but cursing a lot around her still struck him as wrong.

"What are you saying?" his aunt pressed.

"He's got expenses, and he needs those covered. Mostly, I think he just wants to help out the city and the police, even when he's busy. Before I thought he was just a badass who did it for the money, but after everything I've seen and the way he's treated me, the boys, and the neighborhood, I know he cares, even if he sometimes acts like he doesn't."

"That's good to hear. That's *very* good to hear. I guess my first impression was right."

Trey continued scrolling through potential jobs. Las Vegas was filled with low-level scum with bounties. He half-wondered if some of the bounties were sponsored indirectly by organized crime groups who didn't like the freelance competition.

His aunt slipped into a chair beside him and glanced at his phone. Her eyes narrowed.

"You should go after the one on the top," she declared.

Trey frowned, and he stared at the scarred face and shaved head on the screen. "Bruno Smith, level two?" He tapped on the man's picture. Assaults and murders all over the Southwest. The man liked to keep busy. He looked back at his aunt. "Why him? These guys are all garbage."

"I recognize him. That mean SOB likes to go after homeless people. He doesn't kill us, thank God, but he likes to beat us down. I think it's like a game to him."

"You ain't homeless anymore, Aunt Charlyce."

She gave Trey a slight nod. "I… Well, that bastard knocked some teeth out of a friend of mine last winter. Told him if he went to the cops he'd come back and finish him. We figured out where he lived, so we just avoided going around there."

Trey stood up. "You know what the most annoying part of this job is?"

"No, what?"

"Tracking these guys down. If you know where he lives, this'll be easy money." Trey marched over to the closet. "Grab anything you need. We might not be back here for a few hours."

Aunt Charlyce frowned. "Wait. Why would I be going? I'm not a bounty hunter."

"You know where the guy lives and you've got local street knowledge, and I might need that when I'm going after him. Also, I just realized what the Brownstone Agency really needs."

"What?"

"A new administrative assistant." Trey opened the closet, strapped on his holster, and fished out his cuffs. "The big man hates complicated stuff. He's already got an HR firm helping us with the hiring, so having another employee to handle administrative stuff is right up his alley." He slid his coat on before walking out, not even checking to see if she was following.

His aunt wiped a tear away and stepped through the door after him. A home, a job, and a nephew on a good path. She couldn't ask for anything more.

Tyler moved from behind the bar to the front as a new customer sat down; a mousy-looking woman. He kept a smile on his face, though he was a little surprised. Men always outnumbered women in the Black Sun, and the women who did come naturally sorted into hot babes or tough chicks who could rip a man's balls off.

This woman, with her floral sundress, light brown hair, and black glasses, had more of a girl-next-door vibe. He half-wondered if she was a lost tourist who wandered into the first bar she'd spotted. She wasn't ugly, but something about the whole package wasn't doing it for Tyler.

"What'll it be?" he inquired.

"A White Russian," the woman replied. There was nothing sultry or noteworthy about her voice.

She scanned the bar with a curious expression on her face. "Rough crowd."

Tyler added vodka to a glass before responding, "I don't judge people. Everyone's got to have a place to drink."

The woman chuckled. "True enough." She nodded at a cop sitting in the corner. "More than a few cops here, so I guess I shouldn't be too worried."

The bartender added coffee liqueur to the glass. "Yeah, this place is kind of…neutral ground."

"Neutral ground?"

"Cops and people who like to pay less attention to the law at times."

The woman smirked. "You mean criminals?"

"All a matter of perspective."

She leaned in. "Anyone really interesting ever stop by?"

Tyler narrowed his eyes. There was one type of woman who might not fit in at the Black Sun but still risk coming. Time to figure out if the new arrival was one of those.

He finished mixing her drink and set it in front of her.

"Sure, but before you ask, Brownstone isn't here. He almost never comes here, and from what I've heard he's out of town."

The woman's lips parted in surprise. Tyler didn't bother to stop his smirk. Nothing like surprising someone with his grasp of information and psychology. He never got tired of the feeling of superiority.

The woman forced a smile. "Why would you tell me that?"

Yeah, you didn't deny looking for him, now did you? Now I know you were *looking for him.*

"The new bunnies in my place who don't know what the Black Sun is always turn out to be Brownstone groupies." He snorted. "That stuck-up arrogant prick."

The woman laughed softly. "I wouldn't say I'm a Brownstone groupie, but I *do* find the man interesting. He's famous, after all, for his exploits."

"He's a dick. I hope some bounty caps his ass when he's on the toilet someday."

"That would be…a colorful way to die."

"Hey, Tyler," a man called from down the bar. "What's a man got to do to get a damned refill around here?"

The bartender was about to ask Kathy to handle it, but saw that she was already preparing drinks for other customers.

"I'll be right back." Tyler offered the woman a polite nod before heading to the thirsty and far-too-sober customer.

Seconds turned into minutes, and by the time he glanced back at the front of the bar the woman was gone, her White Russian already polished off.

"Fucking Brownstone groupies," Tyler muttered under his breath.

He smiled once he noticed Lieutenant Hall making her way through the front door and to the bar.

The cop took a seat. "Just a Coke. No rum." She held a tablet in her hand.

"Still fighting the good fight, Lieutenant?"

"Yeah." Lieutenant Hall glared at him. "Since someone won't give up information." Her expression softened. "But I will say that the other thing I asked you about is working out, so thanks."

"Whatever I can do to help out my local AET team."

She smirked. "Get my drink ready. Have to hit the ladies' room first."

As the lieutenant turned, Tyler got a glimpse of a webpage opened on her tablet. He couldn't make out a lot in the few seconds of visibility, but what he saw was more than enough.

Level-five bounty, Tessa Vansant.

He knew the name. He'd heard she was coming into town before the cops, after all. What he hadn't known before was what she'd looked like: a plain brunette with glasses. Unless Tessa had a twin sister, she'd downed a White Russian in his bar just before Lieutenant Hall's arrival.

Tyler sighed.

No wonder nothing was stirring down south. My dick must have known she was a psycho.

He snickered. At least that meant she wasn't a Brownstone groupie.

James sat on the hotel bed and scrolled through a few reports the police had sent over. He'd been worried about them coming after him, but instead, they were bending the rules to give him access to additional information so he could better track the bounty.

He needed whatever help he could get, given that Las Vegas wasn't his town. His local contacts were limited to barbeque experts, not information brokers or researchers.

His phone rang, and to his surprise it was Alison.

"Hey, kid," James answered. "Break up with any new boys in the last few days?"

Alison groaned. "No." He swore he could hear the eye roll. "I wanted to make sure you know I'm okay with all that. I mean, not tonight. I went out with three girls from my school to a concert."

"And did those girls bring any boys along?"

"No. It was just a girls' night." She let out a contented sigh. "But it was super-fun. No big magic or stress or anything, just a concert."

"That sounds good. You should do more of that."

"Go to concerts?"

"Go to concerts without boys."

Alison laughed. "It wasn't like it was a girls-only concert, Dad. There were a lot of boys and men there."

James' voice became a growl. "Did any of them talk to you?"

"No. Remember, you're supposed to be calmer about this?"

"I think I just promised to be less intimidating next time I visited the school, but I'm not even at the school."

"You're hopeless."

James grunted. "Have to be me."

A few beats of silence ticked by, and he worried he'd pissed her off.

"Dad, I have to be honest. That isn't why I called."

"Why?"

"I heard on the news that you're in Las Vegas and you might be involved in a job there."

James took several deep breaths. Alison needed to see him for her lie-detection ability to work, but given everything she'd gone through, there was no reason to try and shield her from the harsh realities of the world they lived in.

"Yeah. I didn't come here for that; I came here for Jessie Rae's. But it seems like everybody from Trey's aunt to the cops were itching for me to get involved."

"Trey has an aunt?"

"Long story. Anyway, this bounty—he's bad news. Killing people in front of their kids. Might even have killed a little girl the first time if she hadn't been out of reach."

Alison gasped. "Is she okay?"

"Yeah, she's with CPS now."

"But you're going to make sure she is safe, right, Dad?"

James grunted. "That's right, honey. I sure am, by whatever means necessary."

"That doesn't mean you shouldn't be careful."

"This guy isn't a big deal. He's just a level four."

James hadn't brought his amulet, but he didn't worry about needing it. If the bounty were a true threat, the asshole wouldn't be hiding in the shadows so much.

Alison sighed. "Promise me you'll be careful."

"Yeah. I'll be careful, but that doesn't mean I'm not taking this guy down."

"I never thought you wouldn't," Alison offered quietly. "I just want you to know that I'm proud of you, Dad. You saved me, and you save so many people."

"I'm just a bounty hunter."

"You forget, I can see your soul."

James stared at the phone. "Even from far away?"

"Maybe," the girl replied in a sing-song voice. "But it doesn't matter, because I've seen it before. I know how beautiful it is, and I'm glad that you're adopting me." She sniffled. "I...I've got to go. Talk to you later, Dad. I love you."

"I love you too, Alison."

She ended the call.

Something stung in the corner of his eye. James reached up and wiped away something as rare as him not liking barbeque: a tear.

"Love isn't simple, but it's worth it."

James took a few deep breaths before rising from the hotel bed.

Maybe God's guiding me around to help orphans in a way only I can. Father McCartney would probably say so. Don't know about that, but I know this asshole's going down. Just need to find him.

He nodded once and scrolled through his contacts until he found the number he needed. The phone rang on the other end several times.

"Mr. Brownstone," Peyton offered in a cheerful tone. "I'm guessing you're calling because you want to donate to the Save-The-Peyton Charity Fund? Don't worry, all donations, while not tax-deductible, come with free information attached."

"Yeah, got a few questions."

B ile rose in Detective West's throat. He'd worked a lot of murder scenes in his time in homicide, but it was going to require a lot of whiskey to wash the last week from his mind.

He knelt next to a severed arm surrounded by rifle casings. They hadn't found any weapons in the warehouse, but the three men had obviously been involved in a serious firefight before their deaths. Their killer must have taken the weapons with him.

Detective Lafayette stood over a corpse missing most of its throat. It looked like an animal tore the flesh away. "You think this is our boy?"

"Guys chopped up?" Detective West pointed toward the corpse near the other cop. "Guys who look like someone ate them?" He shook his head. "Yeah, I'm doubting that we're such a freaky city that we're going to get two weird-ass killers so close together like this. I'm sure once forensics examines the bodies, they'll probably find bone particles in the wounds like they did with the parents. Nah, I'm confident we can add another three deaths to our boy's list."

The other cop circled the body as a crime scene photographer took photos. "This doesn't fit the MO, though. No kids involved, and I doubt these guys were just hanging out in a random warehouse. Judging by these shell casings, they were packing assault rifles. Not exactly the tourist crowd."

"Well-dressed thugs with guns? Connected, maybe?"

Detective Lafayette frowned down at another corpse. "Something feels slightly off. I guess we'll run their faces by the organized crime unit and see if they get any hits. The question is what they were doing here."

"You don't show up with that kind of hardware unless you're expecting serious trouble."

"Hunting then? But hunting what?"

"Our boy, I'm guessing."

"Bounty hunters, maybe? They thought they had him, but he turned the tables on them."

Detective West reached into a man's pocket with a gloved hand and fished out a wallet. He opened it. "Well, whoever killed them didn't seem to care about making sure we didn't know who they were. Got a driver's license in here and a business card. No licensed bounty hunter ID card."

"What's the business card say?"

"Yeah, this poor sucker was, according to this, a 'security specialist' with Anders Laboratory."

Detective Lafayette shrugged. "Never heard of them."

"Well, it wouldn't hurt to pay them a little visit. I'm

doubting this is a coincidence." Detective West shook his head.

"What're you thinking?"

"I'm thinking someone tried to play God but ended up closer to the Devil."

Lance stomped down the street, glaring at random people along the way. He enjoyed seeing them move to the side, or in some cases, head to the other side of the street entirely. It was good to be back in Vegas after his vacation in Hawaii.

He'd hated the place. Too much water. Too pretty. Too many people trying too hard to be relaxed. Give him a place like Vegas anytime. The energy invigorated him, and the harsh desert sun made him feel alive.

Living in Hawaii made people soft. They had fucking paradise handed to them, but Las Vegas was a city carved out of the heart of the desert. It shouldn't exist, but it did. It was a monument to man's ability to rule over nature.

A man met Lance's gaze and quickly scurried off.

Lance didn't give two shits if people thought he was a dick. He was a class-four bounty hunter, which meant he was an officially-certified badass, and if people had a problem with it, they could move to another fucking city or kick his ass to prove he was a pussy.

Vegas is mine, bitches.

A man in a worn trench coat and sunglasses stepped out of a nearby alley. The poor fucker had some sort of skin condition, judging by the leathery skin covering his face and his tight mottled flesh. Maybe the fucker was dying.

The bounty hunter couldn't help it. He laughed.

The man looked his way. "Problem?" His voice sounded hollow and ragged, like he'd been drinking acid every day for years.

"You're just one ugly son of a bitch. Don't flash me, please." Lance laughed and held up a hand. He didn't know anyone funnier than him.

The man grinned, his incisors prominent, his blackened teeth in need of more than a little cleaning. An acid wash perhaps.

"Oh, I've no intention of drawing people's eyes to me quite yet in a place like this. Not in this way. There is…a proper way to do things. People should know fear, but it must be orchestrated."

"You need to find some hot babes first before you show 'em your shriveled-up dick?"

"You're an ignorant fool." The leathery-faced man sneered. "I'd kill you, but it's not yet time." He looked Lance up and down. "And you're not worthy of assimilation."

The bounty hunter scoffed. "Yeah, I'm so fucking scared of some fucking flasher bum from an alley." He flipped the man off. "Enjoy starving to death, you piece of shit." He continued up the street.

"If there's one thing I won't do," the man called after him, "it's starve."

Lance glanced over his shoulder. The man had removed his sunglasses and was now staring at him with glowing red eyes.

Fuck, so now we not only have to deal with homeless bums, we've got to deal with homeless bums from Oriceran?

The bounty hunter grunted. This wasn't fun anymore, and kicking some bum's ass in public might get the police on him. He wasn't going to risk his license for a few minutes of fun.

If he ever saw that fucker in a dark alley, though, all bets were off.

A half-block up, Lance found a bar and pushed inside. He sat on a stool and ordered a beer before pulling out his phone to scan for local bounties. Vacation was over, and it was time get back to work.

Lance checked the new bounty alerts first.

"Red Eyes Killer?" he murmured to himself. He clicked on the bounty and read the details. "Son of a bitch." He leapt from the stool and sprinted for the door.

"What about your beer?" the bartender called.

"Fuck the beer. It's probably watered-down anyway."

Lance threw open the door and ran down the street looking for the red-eyed man in the trench coat, but he was nowhere.

"Where the fuck is he?" He hurried toward the nearest alley and peered down it. Still no Red Eyes Killer. "Shit, shit, shit."

The bounty hunter punched a wall. "Next time, I'll just fucking beat any freak down and ask questions later."

Trey parked his F-350 near a bridge under a dry wash. "Wait in the truck." He patted the glove box. "There's a backup pistol in there in case anyone comes to bother you."

"Be careful, Trey."

He grinned. "You should be saying that to the other guy."

The bounty hunter stepped out of his truck and carefully closed the door. They'd stopped to talk to a few other street people, and they'd all pointed Trey and his aunt to this bridge. He fished out his flashlight. The few street lights in the distance weren't enough to push away the shadows cloaking the area.

Bruno was on the hunt tonight. That was what everyone had said, and he'd be hunting around the bridge. People had tried to get the word out so everyone could avoid the area.

Trey snorted as he made his way toward the bridge. Bruno was the worst sort of man. Kicking the ass of someone who got in your face or came after you was one thing, but beating people down who were already on the bottom of the heap was the act of a coward. It proved nothing other than the man was a fucking piece of shit who needed to go down.

Wind howled underneath the bridge, and Trey searched around for any movement in the deep shadows.

"Well, well, well," called a voice from underneath the bridge. A muscled, shaven-head man stepped out right into the path of Trey's light. "I was starting to get a little bored. I thought you little homeless parasites had scurried off and I'd have to go find some street whore to rough up."

"You're a real piece of work."

"I'm not a parasite like you, you piece of shit."

Trey scoffed and pointed his flashlight at his suit. "Does this look like the kind of thing a homeless man wears, motherfucker?"

Bruno laughed. "Ah, sorry, pal. A lot of those fuckers are around here." He shrugged. "What the fuck are you doing out here?" He grinned. "Hey, you want to join the hunt? It's fun if you've never tried it. Nothing feels as good as some parasite's nose cracking under your knuckles."

"You're talking about beating the shit out of people?"

"Yeah. It's fun, and the little fuckers are too afraid of the police to report anything. It's a victimless crime." Bruno shrugged.

Trey gritted his teeth, wondering about the kinds of assholes who'd preyed on his aunt through the last seven years. "Homeless people are still people, motherfucker."

Bruno shook his head. "Oh, some sort of fucking bleeding heart? Is that why you're here? To give them a blanket and a hot meal?" He spat on the ground.

"Nah, nothing like that."

"Then who are you?"

Trey smirked. "I'm just your not-so-local level three bounty hunter, motherfucker. I'm Trey Garfield. I'm from Los Angeles, and I work for the Brownstone Agency."

The other man's smile faltered. "Brownstone Agency, as in James Brownstone?"

"Yeah, you piece of shit. The big man is my boss." Trey fluffed his jacket. "But we don't need Mr. Brownstone for a worthless piece of crap like you."

Bruno stepped forward, cracking his knuckles. "What, am I supposed to be afraid of you?"

"I don't give a shit if you're afraid or not, but I'm not afraid of you."

Trey almost wanted to laugh at the insulted look that went across the bounty's face.

Bruno regained control and sneered. "If you're here for me then you've seen my record. You know I've killed people."

The bounty hunter shrugged. "Yeah, and when I looked closer at it, what I found was you're a coward who likes to pick on people a lot smaller and weaker than you, which means you ain't used to fighting someone strong." Trey gestured around him. "Which is why you're here in the middle of the night looking to beat up some homeless old man. Bitch, *please*. I'm more afraid of my ex-girlfriend than your weak ass. Bring it, bitch. Show me what you've got."

Bruno yelled and charged Trey. The bounty hunter dodged to the side and slammed his elbow into the man's head. His flashlight dropped to the ground.

The criminal collapsed to his knees with a grunt.

Trey clapped. "Yeah. It's hard when it's not some starving old man on the street now, isn't it, bitch."

Bruno grunted and pushed himself up. Trey threw several quick punches into his head. The thud of flesh on flesh echoed underneath the bridge. The bounty fell back down.

"Fuck, bitch, I wish you had hair to grab," Trey hissed. He grabbed Bruno's head with both hands and slammed his knee into the man's face a few times until the criminal fell to the ground with a groan. He tried to grab Trey's leg.

The bounty hunter kicked the man in the stomach a few times until he rolled to his side, moaning.

Trey rolled the moaning man onto his stomach and handcuffed him. "We at the Brownstone Agency try to keep it professional, which is why I'm not beating the shit out of you now that I've got you all cuffed, but that doesn't mean I didn't enjoy kicking the shit out of you before." He patted the man on his head. "Like I said, bitch, you ain't used to dealing with someone strong." He rolled Bruno back over. "I hope you enjoy prison, Bruno."

His face battered, the man glared at Trey. A grin split his face, and he laughed.

Trey narrowed his eyes. "What's so fucking funny, asshole?"

Bruno spit out blood. "I'm just thinking about all the shit I'm gonna do to you once I've got you on the ground. I'm *not* a professional, fuckwad. I'm gonna beat you way harder than I ever beat any piece-of-shit homeless parasite."

A gunshot blasted through the quiet night.

"Ouch, motherfucker!" screamed someone from behind Trey.

What the fuck?

The bounty hunter spun and spotted a man with a 2x4 at his feet clutching his arm. Trey tackled the new guy and knocked his ass out with two clean punches.

He pulled out his reserve cuffs and secured the second man before yanking out his gun and spinning back toward Bruno.

The flashlight still on the ground pointed past the cuffed criminal and highlighted the slender silhouette of a woman. After a few seconds Trey recognized Aunt Charlyce, gun in hand.

Trey holstered his pistol. "I thought I told you to stay in the truck."

"You're my nephew, and ain't no one gonna touch my nephew if I can stop it."

The bounty hunter grinned. "Well, you saved my ass." He winked down at Bruno. "Keep dreaming about all shit you were gonna to do me, Bruno. You can dream about it all the time you're in fucking prison."

15

"This doesn't look creepy at all," Detective West murmured as the cops' car pulled up to the gate. He'd been expecting Anders Laboratory to be some tiny facility tucked away in a nice part of town, but instead, it was built at the base of a mountain on the edge of town.

His partner shrugged. "Maybe they wanted to keep it away from anything in case of an accident."

"Like a red-eyed magical killer getting loose?"

"Yeah, exactly like that."

Detective West stopped and rolled down his window. He pulled out his badge and ID to show to the security guard.

"Detective West. I called ahead."

The security guard nodded and pressed a button in his guard post. "I'll let them know you're here."

The metal gates blocking further passage parted with a groan.

A couple more minutes brought the detective to a small

parking lot. Now that they had reached the building, they could see that Anders Laboratory wasn't as small as it had appeared from a distance. The white facade with glass windows stretching to the roof was part of a larger complex that extended into the mountain. The scientists could have countless levels carved into the ground, as far as the cop knew.

"Yeah, this gets weirder by the second," Detective West mumbled.

His partner nodded. "I checked into them. Not a huge amount of information, but they do have a license for dangerous hardcore shit. Like germ warfare shit."

"Great. I'll sleep better knowing that."

The cops filed out of their car and made their way to the front entrance. Two smiling men in business suits stood in the open doorway, and they motioned the detectives inside.

One of them, an older man with silver hair, offered his hand. "I'm Doctor Anders, and this is one of my chief researchers, Doctor Simmons."

The detectives shook the men's hands.

White tile paved the massive entrance foyer. A front reception desk manned by a tense-looking woman was the only thing breaking up the room, other than a few white chairs near the entrance.

Doctor Anders motioned to the chairs. "Please take a seat."

Detective West glanced at a chair. "You want to talk here?"

The scientist sighed. "We have many projects under non-disclosure agreements, both governmental and private. We can't proceed farther into the facility without going through a number of legal procedures, which would take time."

The two detectives sat, and the scientists followed.

Detective West glanced at the two men. Years of being a cop had given him great insight into body language. A man's face screamed he was guilty long before his body, but these men didn't seem afraid. They didn't rub their hands or touch their faces. Didn't shift in their seats.

If anything, the faint frowns they were barely concealing spoke to something else entirely: annoyance, as if taking a few minutes out of their day to assist a murder investigation was a burden.

The detective cleared his throat. "As I told you over the phone, we found three mutilated corpses in a warehouse in central Vegas. Information in their wallets linked them to your facility."

Doctor Anders nodded. "I don't handle low-level personnel management, but I did check with HR, and they verified that the three men worked security for our facility."

Doctor Simmons frowned but didn't say anything.

"I see. Do you have any idea why they'd be in a ware-house in central Vegas with assault rifles?"

Doctor Anders shrugged and looked at Doctor Simmons. "Assault rifles? Well, they *are* security personnel. I'm sure they are trained with all sorts of weapons. Doctor Simmons?"

"I wouldn't have the foggiest idea. I didn't work closely with security."

Detective West nodded to his partner. Sometimes

changing the interrogator could help, even going beyond Good Cop/Bad Cop.

"These guys...were chopped up," Detective Lafayette explained. "Limbs cut clean off their bodies. One of the guys had been...partially eaten."

"Eaten?" Doctor Anders echoed. "Well, I suppose there are rats and that sort of thing."

"Yeah, well, these would have to had to be some big rats."

"Maybe they snuck over from Oriceran." Doctor Anders chuckled, as did Doctor Simmons.

"So you're saying you have no idea what these men would have been doing there? Chasing something, perhaps?"

"I can assure you that we have no idea."

"You said you have a lot of government contracts here," Detective West mentioned, breaking in. "So I'm assuming you perform extensive background checks on all your employees?"

"Of course."

"Would you mind sharing them with us?"

Doctor Anders sighed. "I hate to be difficult, Detective, but not without a warrant. There's a privacy issue involved, and I don't want our employees feeling like the information they've agreed to share will go to just whoever."

"Not to 'whoever.' To the cops."

"I'm sorry, but this is an elite facility. You probably couldn't pass our background check."

Detective West's face twitched. "What kind of research do you do here?"

"I'm sorry, but we really can't talk about that. NDAs, you understand."

"Is it possible that something escaped from here?"

Doctor Anders laughed, and Doctor Simmons joined him.

Detective West shrugged.

"What's so funny?" Detective Lafayette inquired.

"Oh, it's we just don't do the kind of work you're thinking. It's all microbes and that sort of thing. If something escaped," he made air quotes around the word, "we'd know instantly. We have numerous air sensors monitoring for that sort of thing."

"We're talking something bigger. Something man-sized."

The scientists exchanged annoyed looks again before Doctor Anders responded. "Man-sized? Microbes... Well, they're *microbes*. They don't get even insect-sized."

"You follow the news at all?"

Doctor Anders frowned, apparently taken off-guard. "I find it's mostly trivia for the masses."

"A killer is stalking the streets of Las Vegas, a red-eyed killer with magical powers. We think it is responsible for killing your men. Our forensic analysis found unidentified bone particles in some of the wounds, both at the warehouse and some of the other sites. DNA testing suggests human origin, but there are some differences. I don't... understand all of them, but there's some evidence that whatever it is isn't fully human. The lab isn't really sure. They've never seen anything like it."

Doctor Anders crossed his arms and leaned back. "That

is fascinating." He looked at Doctor Simmons. "Can you imagine something like that?"

The other scientist shrugged. "I think I can solve the mystery of our men at least, Detective."

Detective West nodded. He'd hoped mentioning the forensic evidence would get their tongues moving, but he'd expected to have to work them a bit more.

The cops both leaned forward, eagerness on their faces.

The scientist cleared his throat. "I imagine they were driving to or from work. Many of our security men here are quite conscientious. Perhaps they saw your strange semi-human killer and decided to go after it." He clucked his tongue. "It's an unfortunate loss, I suppose. This is why people should leave that sort of thing to law enforcement or bounty hunters."

Detective West's hands squeezed into fists. "You're both saying that you don't think this has anything to do with your lab?"

"I can't see how it would. Germ hunters don't use rifles."

"Maybe some germ you fucked with changed someone."

Doctor Anders laughed. "You've watched too many movies, Detective. If you want strange changes, go talk to an Oriceran or a wizard." He glanced down at his watch. "I hate to cut this short, but since this doesn't actually seem to relate to our lab directly, both Doctor Simmons and I have things to attend to."

"Fine," the detective agreed through gritted teeth. "If you find anything we should know about, please let us know."

Doctors Anders and Simmons stood.

"Of course, detectives." Doctor Anders nodded toward the door. "I'm sure you can see yourselves out." With that both the scientists turned toward the elevator.

Detective West and his partner made their way outside before he spoke again. "Did you notice there was a complete lack of sympathy for their dead employees?"

Detective Lafayette nodded. "It's like it was an annoying inconvenience to them, but I don't think we're going to get a warrant just because those guys worked here."

"Yeah. Not yet, but it's a start."

James sat at a table in the back of the bar, not sure who looked more threatening: him, or the two men already present.

Nothing approaching fear entered his mind, but he didn't want to have to get into a fight and risk his chance to get information. Red Eyes needed his ass kicked as soon as possible, and every minute the bounty hunter spent gathering information was another minute his prey could be killing someone.

One of them, a short man with blood-shot eyes, looked him over. "Here you are in the flesh, James Brownstone."

The bounty hunter shrugged. "You Tim?"

"That's what I'm going by today." The man sneered. "And that's all you need to know, but I'm impressed that you were able to track me down."

"I know people. They tell me things."

The other man chuckled. "But you don't know enough people or things, which is why you're here, right?"

James shrugged. "My friends tell me that you're the man to talk to if someone needs to know what's happening on the street around here, and I need to know."

Tim gave James a lopsided grin. "Yeah, I guess that's true, but why the fuck should I help you? I don't like your type." The man narrowed his eyes. "And if you try to threaten my ass, I'm walking right out of here and bullets will be flying."

The other man at the table's hand drifted toward a suspicious bulge in his jacket.

James grunted. If he were in LA he'd know how hard he could push, but tossing a man through a window to make a point probably wouldn't get him the information he needed in a timely manner.

"I don't want trouble. I just want information, and I can pay."

The bounty hunter locked eyes with Tim. James might not want to throw threats around, but he wasn't leaving this bar until he got the information he needed. A monster walked the streets, and it was time for a little alien-enhanced-ass-kicking.

Tim nodded to his silent friend. The second man rose and headed toward the bar, the swish of his jacket revealing his gun.

He nodded at James. "I got information, Brownstone, but that doesn't mean I'm going to give it to you without a good reason."

"Good reason? You must have already heard that I'm looking for the Red Eyes Killer."

Tim shrugged. "I hear a lot of things. So, what, am I supposed to be impressed?"

"How the fuck is that not a good reason? This guy isn't making business opportunities for drug dealers or some shit. This is a fucker butchering innocent people in front of children. Even a guy like you has to have some lines you think shouldn't be crossed."

The other man's face darkened. "Not saying this guy is on my list of favorite people, but business is business. I'm not running a charity here."

"Those on the street know the score, and I'm just trying to get someone who kills off the street so you won't be bothered. Eventually, this guy's gonna try and take it beyond killing random parents. He'll fuck with people like you or your contacts. Come on, we both know that guys who think they are tough shit like to go after underworld people to make a point."

"True." Tim rubbed his chin. "I still want ten thousand for my trouble."

James snorted. "Even though I'm trying to stop a serial killer?"

"Can't buy beer with good intentions, Brownstone, and I don't do community service. It's only because this guy's a piece of shit that I'm willing to help you at all."

James nodded. "Fine. I'll pay what you want. You should know I'm good for it." His hands curled into fists, and he still wanted to throw the man through a window.

Tim grinned. "Glad we could do business. I'll tell everyone that you're a reasonable guy when it comes down to it." He looked around at the room before focusing on James again. "He's been on the move. From what I hear, people have been seeing him in Rancho Charleston."

"Are you sure it's him? Maybe people are just freaking out."

"Not a lot of red-eyed freaks around with weird skin, even in Las Vegas."

James frowned. "And how come the cops can't find him?"

"Come on, Brownstone, you're a bounty hunter. You should know."

James shrugged. "Why don't you tell me?"

"I'm not like a lot of guys. I've got no beef with the police. We all have our roles. The thing is, though, the police—they're reactive, not proactive." Tim laughed. "And this is America. We like that shit. We don't want the police all up in our faces asking us about shit we haven't even done yet."

"This is a murder investigation, though. It's not about being proactive."

"Nope, but it *is* about limited money and priorities. I'm just saying they aren't plugged into the underbelly of the city like I am. Plenty of people out there who don't want attention, but see things like Red Eyes in Rancho Charleston. They talk to me, but avoid the cops."

James narrowed his eyes. "If people know where he is, why hasn't anyone gone after him?"

"Why risk your life when someone like the cops or James Brownstone is going to do it?" Tim shook his head. "There's a guy out there, Little Blue. I've set up a meeting. Let him know that Simon sent you and he'll help you out."

"Simon? But your name is Tim!"

The other man laughed. "I was high when I set that shit up, and Little Blue. Well, he's particular, you see. He doesn't like it when people change things." He stood. "Good luck, Brownstone. I hope you find this Red Eyes guy and take him out. I'll be in touch for my money."

The F-350 rumbled along the streets of Las Vegas. Little Blue had filled James in on a few more sightings of Red Eyes. He was struck by how the killer seemed to be hiding from some people, but all but announcing his presence to others. So far no one who'd spotted Red Eyes had seen him recently enough for it to be useful, but at least their sightings established that the man was still in the area.

Rancho Charleston wasn't that big an area, and tracking the asshole down was moving from the improbable to the likely column.

Guess it's a good thing I brought my guns, knives, and that grenade, even if I didn't bring the amulet.

Taking on a level four without the protection of his amulet would be a risk, but the fact that Red Eyes was still hiding suggested that the killer lacked the raw power of someone like King Pyro. If all else failed, James would just cut the guy's head off. That worked most of the time.

James had hunted enough bounties to see that there

was some sort of pattern underlying Red Eyes' movements, probably something about the killer trying to make a show of his strength. But at the same time, murdering parents in front of their kids didn't do much to prove the man was an ass-kicker.

Maybe I'm wrong, and I shouldn't think about it too hard. The guy's probably just a fucking psycho. Or maybe it's about strength and fear.

James pulled his truck over to the curb. A few gang members lingered near a building, smoking joints.

The bounty hunter killed his engine, then stepped out and made his way over to the gang members.

One of them looked up from his joint. "You're fucking James Brownstone, right?"

"Yeah," James rumbled. "Little Blue told me about some people who might have seen the Red Eyes Killer." He reached into his jacket.

The gang members all whipped out their guns.

James snorted and pulled out his wallet. "If I wanted your asses, this already would have been over."

"Maybe we'll just jack your wallet, bitch."

James shook his head and glared at the men. "I've been itching to put someone through a wall the last few days, so go ahead and try. Or you can get a little cash to help track down a fucking serial killer."

The gang members exchanged looks before putting their guns away.

James fished out a few large bills as a donation to the local gang and handed them over.

The gang member shrugged. "Actually, one of our guys mentioned seeing him just a couple hours ago." He pointed up the street. "We're staying clear of that fucker. I don't mess with magic shit."

"I do. Where was he seen?"

"Go four blocks north and one block west. That's where he saw him, coming out of an alley near a bar there."

"You sure it was him?"

"Nope, but it was some weird-looking fucker we haven't seen around."

"Thanks," James rumbled.

The bounty hunter made his way back to his truck. He wasn't going to risk these assholes deciding to test their bravery by stealing his ride. He didn't have time to teach the Las Vegas underworld a lesson.

The F-350 roared away from the dope smokers and down the street as James followed the gang member's directions. He finally spotted the alley near the bar and parked the truck.

A metallic scent assaulted his nose before he'd even stepped into the alley. He'd spilled enough blood to recognize the scent immediately.

James whipped out his .45 and crept into the alley. Blood heavily splattered the walls on either side for several yards, where the headless corpse of a large man lay on its back. The poor asshole's arms and legs had been cut off and strewn across the alley.

"Yeah, this looks like my guy," he muttered.

After taking a few more steps into the alley, James spotted the head. The dead man's face was fixed in wide-eyed surprise. Even mangled, he recognized the man's face from a few bounty hunting articles.

It was Lance Johnasen, a class-four bounty hunter based out of Vegas.

James grunted. The man's death proved that Red Eyes was tough enough to take out more than surprised parents. That meant it was only a matter of time before everyone in Vegas was in danger.

He whipped out his phone. Detectives West and Lafayette needed to know about the latest kill.

"Sorry, pal. I'll get him for both of us."

After chatting with the police James continued to search the nearby area, hoping that Red Eyes was sticking around to admire his handiwork and he might get lucky. A frustrating hour into his search his phone rang with a call from Shay.

"Hey, Shay," he answered.

She yawned on the other end. "What group?"

"Huh?"

"What large group of criminals are you going after? I've seen a few alerts about you going after some bounties in Vegas, but I'm guessing there's more to it than that. You shouldn't be cleaning out those kinds of people without my help."

"Nah, it's nothing like that. It's just one bounty, a level four. He's a twisted fuck, but I'm not that worried, even without my amulet."

"Seriously? There aren't a dozen? Or a hundred?"

James grunted. "Just one."

"Well, good, then I don't have to run back from Asia.

My first location didn't really work out, so I'm having to check out a new place. Probably be gone another week. I was kind of worried about you being bored, but it looks like you found a way to entertain yourself. Wait, why were you in Las Vegas to begin with?"

James chuckled. "I'm just in Vegas chasing down a bounty and eating barbeque."

"Jessie Rae's. Of course. Just make sure you brush your teeth a lot when you get home. I don't like the taste of barbeque sauce when I kiss you. I know, I'll just make you brush your teeth every time you want to kiss me. That'll do it." She laughed and smacked her lips in a pale imitation to a kiss. "Talk to you later. Don't die."

"I'll try not to, but no promises."

"Such a sweet-talker." Shay ended the call.

James stared at his phone for a moment, wondering if Shay was joking about the teeth brushing or not.

"If that shit's true, it's going to be a pain the ass."

***

Tessa chuckled to herself as she strolled through the farmers' market booths. Vegetables, fruit, and handicrafts—all so banal and peaceful.

She was glad she'd decided to catch up on the news. If she hadn't, she would have never known that James Brownstone was in Las Vegas. For all his strength and skills the man couldn't teleport, which meant he was hours away from his home city. And, he was already on the trail of another killer.

This meant she had a rare opportunity to have some

fun and prove she was alive in Los Angeles, and it'd been far too long since Tessa had done that.

People streamed back and forth murmuring to each other, laughing, and carrying items in a variety of bags. No, not people, *ghosts*, she reminded herself.

You're not alive. That's why you're here, trying to find something to remind your souls of what it means to live.

Tessa pulled her emerald-tipped wand from her purse and smiled.

A few people nearby eyed her, but there was no fear in their eyes.

She didn't care. The fear of ghosts pretending to be people was irrelevant. The only thing important was that she proved her strength and her existence.

The witch made several precise movements with her wand and started chanting in Sumerian. Even though she didn't care about fear, she enjoyed the looks of confusion on the faces of people nearby. Several stopped to watch her.

If they started running, they might have some small chance of surviving. Their lingering curiosity would be their doom.

They're already dead, and they just won't accept it. I'll prove to them what they are.

Two pulsating glyphs appeared in the air. People nearby actually started clapping. Tessa laughed.

The rays of light forming the glyphs swirled and twisted around each other and cheering joined the clapping.

"Enjoy the show!" the witch yelled. "Hope you like the Rabisu!"

The roar of the crowd intensified as the light lingered and began to form the outline of huge bodies. The light faded and revealed two giants covered with green scales. Their long arms were covered with sharp black protrusions, and they stared at the crowd with green and yellow vertical pupils.

The cheers stopped instantly. Confused murmurs replaced them.

The first Rabisu raised its palm and shot a flickering ball of emerald light into a nearby man. He screamed as green fire surrounded him and dropped to the ground, already dead, terror still etched on his scorched face. The smell of his burnt flesh filled the air.

Screams and panic consumed the crowd as everyone bolted. Both Rabisu continued to pitch orbs into the crowd, striking victims indiscriminately.

A brave but foolish man charged Tessa, pulling out a Glock and aiming at her.

"Stop them right now!" he yelled.

Tessa could have had the Rabisu kill the man, but his defiance heightened her sense of life.

"If you want them to stop you need to kill me," the witch explained with a smile. "Prove to me that you're more than a ghost."

The horrible buzzing of the Rabisu's energy blasts filled the air, and smoke poured into the sky from burning stalls.

"Fuck you, witch." The man pulled the trigger.

Tessa jerked backward and laughed, and the pain faded after a second. Green ichor spilled from one of the Rabisu in the identical place she'd been shot, but its wound started to close immediately.

"Try again," the witch suggested. "You're still a ghost."

The man kept firing until a Rabisu blasted him and he collapsed to the ground, dead.

Tessa patted her dress to ensure that the redirection spell had worked. A little wound was annoying enough, but she liked her dress.

Sirens cut through the air.

"Let's see what the police have to offer me."

The witch tapped her wand against her palm as she waited. By this point, everyone else had fled the area or died. A dozen bodies littered the ground as the smoke continued to darken the sky.

She took a deep breath.

"I'm alive." She surveyed the carnage. "I've not killed anyone. I just put down some ghosts who didn't even know they were dead."

The sirens grew closer, and two police cars screeched to a halt.

The Rabisu blasted the first car right after the cops jumped out and the explosions knocked them to the ground. The other cops leapt to the side before the summoned creatures could annihilate their vehicle.

More sirens closed.

Tessa sighed and jogged away from the Rabisu. The tether binding them to this world would dissolve once she was far enough away, but they'd still linger long enough to keep the police's attention on them.

"I am alive," Tessa repeated. "I've proven it, and I've made the world a better place by purging ghosts."

Trey sat at the table in the Aria suite, checking his messages. A banking alert popped up. The police had finished processing the bounty, and the money had been deposited into his account. He grinned, wondering what it'd be like if bounty hunters had to carry big briefcases of cash out of the police department instead.

"Nothing like a good payday. Took these guys a little longer than normal, but I'm not complaining. There's even a little bonus in here I wasn't expecting. Very nice."

His aunt smiled at him from across the table. "That's great, Trey. I'm so proud of you."

"You saved my ass, so I'm gonna give you half."

She shook her head. "You're doing no such thing."

Trey chuckled. "Ain't used to people refusing money when offered. You earned it. If you hadn't been there, who knows what would have happened? Nana would need money for my funeral."

"Your nana didn't teach me to take money from family

when they've done helped me like you have. You're already helping me so much."

"Auntie Charlyce, why you being like this? I want to give you the money. Not saying it's nothing, but it's not like it's my last dime or something, either."

"I'm not trying to make you mad. Look, if you can get me a job with Mr. Brownstone as an administrative assistant, that's fine. I'll work for my living, but you came here, and you saved me. You could have heard what I had to say and still just left me on the streets. You didn't have to offer me a place to live." She motioned around the massive suite. "Or book us a place like this. I owe you so much already, but I'm your aunt. I should be saving you. It's my *job* to save you, not yours to save me." She punctuated her sentence with a slap to the table. "I'm not taking any of that bounty money."

Trey frowned. "You're sure?"

It didn't sit right with him to not reward his aunt for saving his ass, but at the same time, he understood pride. He really didn't want to harm her after she'd just started to claw it back from the darkness of her street life.

"Yeah, I'm sure. Even if you kicked me out right now, if your Mr. Brownstone can help that little angel I can die happy, knowing I did my small part to make the world a better place."

Trey snorted. "There ain't gonna be any dying going on, except for that red-eyed sonofabitch." He blew out a breath. "Enough of that for now, though. You hungry?"

"I'm okay. I can go a long time without eating."

"You're not doing that anymore." He pulled out his

phone and dialed James. "Should check in with the big man anyway."

"Hey, Trey," James rumbled a moment later.

Trey smiled. Even the man's voice was badass. It was like something you'd expect from a giant statue who'd learned how to talk.

"Hey, big man. You take that bitch out yet?"

"Nope. I've narrowed down the area, but I think I'm stuck for now. I barely missed him, and I don't know if I'm gonna find much tonight."

"You'll get him, James. You always do. Hey, you should sit down for some dinner with my Auntie Charlyce and me. Hell, maybe she's good luck. She already helped me bag a bounty."

"Really? Sure, why not? I'm hungry."

"How about seafood?"

"Seafood?" James sounded surprised.

"She loves it." Trey shot a glance at Aunt Charlyce, and she smiled back at him.

The big man grew quiet for a few seconds. Trey snickered, guessing James was disappointed they weren't going for barbeque.

"Sure thing, Trey."

"Okay, I'll figure out a place and text you the address."

About forty-five minutes later, the trio all sat around a table at a decent but not too upscale place. Trey didn't want either his aunt or James feeling out of place.

The junior bounty hunter might have grown up poor,

but he'd yet to encounter a place where he felt uncomfortable. He believed in himself, and he didn't give two shits what stuck-up people thought about him. That confidence made it easy for him to adapt to new situations, and confidence earned respect.

James swallowed a forkful of fish. "At least this place doesn't have a billion different types of forks. A fork is a fu—" He glanced at Aunt Charlyce. "A fork is a fork."

The woman laughed. "I've been living on the streets for seven years. There ain't nothing you can say that will offend me, Mr. Brownstone."

James shrugged. "If you say so."

"Trey told me you said you were close to finding the killer?"

He grunted. "Yeah, but not close enough. He killed someone else, this time a bounty hunter. I've tracked him to the Rancho Charleston area, but haven't been able to find anything else yet. Police are sweeping the area with drones, but they haven't come up with anything either. For all we know, the guy's invisible to drones. That's the problem with magical assholes."

Aunt Charlyce sighed and shook her head. "That monster needs to pay."

James grunted. "Don't worry. I met the daughter of the first victim and promised I'd get this guy."

"You met my little angel? Bless you, Mr. Brownstone." The woman nodded, a look of renewed determination on her face. "I'll reach out to the homeless in that area. No one realizes how much we homeless see. We mind our business and we don't like going to the cops, but that don't mean we don't see."

"You ain't homeless anymore," Trey clarified. "You need to remember that."

She reached over to pat his hand. "I still have contacts, though. Point is, homeless don't like to be noticed, and a lot of people want to ignore them. To a lot of people, homeless are background noise."

James nodded. "I understand. The whole reason I try to spread my rep isn't to be noticed, but to make my job easier." He shrugged. "I like shit simple, and if anything, all this attention makes things harder."

Trey grinned. "Your rep makes *my* job easier, big man. You'd be surprised how many times I bust some punk's door down and say I'm with the Brownstone Agency, and they give up without fighting." He took a sip of water before continuing, "Even when I was still running the gang, that was half the point of my rep. I didn't want trouble. If people knew the gang was strong, they wouldn't come after us. Don't matter how badass you are, some bitch can always get in a lucky hit."

"True enough."

Aunt Charlyce sighed and looked down. "I know about having a bad reputation. I have a past as a junkie, a reputation that's gonna make it hard for me to get a job for a long time. I wonder if I'll be able to live it down."

James pulled out his phone and frowned down at it. He nodded at Trey. "Hey, I need to chat with you in private for a second."

Trey nodded and glanced at his aunt. The pained look on her face stabbed at his heart. "We'll be right back, Auntie."

"Take your time, Trey."

The two bounty hunters made their way outside.

"What's up?" Trey inquired. "You get a hit on Red Eyes?"

"Nah, I was just pretending I got a message to get you out here."

"Huh?" Trey stared at James. This sort of thing was rare for the straightforward bounty hunter.

"Nah. This is more about management."

"I'm not following you."

James nodded toward the restaurant. "Your aunt. You sent me a text about her being an administrative assistant. I hadn't responded."

Trey nodded. "Yeah. I figured you would when you got the time. I know you're busy."

"I've been thinking about it and weighing the pros and cons and shit like that."

"I know you got the HR company doing a lot of that shit, but she could help with typing and even organizing some of the boys. I can't have everybody and their cousin texting and calling me all the time. I need a filter."

"I can see that." James nodded slowly, his face hardening. "But that's not the problem."

Trey's jaw tensed. "What's the problem?"

James stared straight into the other man's eyes with an intensity that made Trey want to turn away. "Don't bullshit me. Straight up, can she work?"

Trey took a deep breath as he thought about the question. He wanted to help Aunt Charlyce, but the last thing he would ever want to do was lie to the man in front of him.

The junior bounty hunter cleared his throat. "She was a

junkie for seven years. She's only been clean about a month."

James grunted. "That's not a long time to be clean."

"Yeah, but she's also been with me. I'm not seeing any twitching or any other shit that tells me she wants to shoot up, so that should count for something."

"That's a good sign, but why the change?"

Trey shrugged. "Lots of reasons, I'm guessing, but from what she said some of it is like you. She found religion."

James chuckled. "I didn't find religion, religion found me. But yeah, I can see how being a little God-fearing could put you on a new path." He furrowed his brow. "I also have to consider some other shit."

"Like what?"

"Like the fact that a homeless former junkie's main concern seems to be getting justice for a little girl she doesn't even know. We wouldn't be on this if she wasn't involved, which means she's trying to be a better person. That's more than I can say for most people."

Trey sighed. "I'm not gonna lie, James. She's family, which means I want to give her a shot, but I also get that my family ain't the most impressive bunch outside of Nana."

"Okay, here's how it's gonna work. This isn't 'three strikes and you're out' for her. It's one strike, but if I didn't trust your judgment I wouldn't have you working for me, and I wouldn't risk my rep on you. So it's your call. Is she our administrative assistant?"

"So, do you think we need one? I mean if you don't, I can take it. She won't want charity. I'm already gonna give her a place to live, but that's a family matter."

"The only reason we haven't fucked up already is that we don't have all your boys hitting the streets for bounties yet. This shit's gonna get complicated. We don't want everybody going after the same guy and that kind of crap, and I don't want to handle it. Do you want to handle it?"

"Hell, no." Trey grinned. "Okay, hiring an administrative assistant sounds good, and I think we should do it."

James shrugged. "Besides, it's either her, someone we don't know, or Shay."

Trey laughed. He hadn't talked with James' woman much, but he knew two things. First, she could beat down his entire gang just as well as her man, and second, James didn't need her busting his balls at the Brownstone Agency.

"I'll test her out while we're working here in Las Vegas. We'll pull out of the Aria and hit some Airbnb for a week. I'll see if she can help hold down the fort while we're working here."

James shook Trey's hand. "Sounds good, now let's get back in there."

Maria gritted her teeth as she surveyed the burned-out stalls and scorched police cars. The bodies had already been removed, but she'd seen the twelve dead civilians when she arrived. This was the exact reason she'd joined AET: to protect people from the kinds of monsters who'd massacre random people going about their day.

And the bitch had gotten away. That was what burned the most.

Sergeant Weber walked up to her. "They're adjusting

her bounty to dead or alive. That should get some guys coming, maybe even Br—"

"Don't fucking say his name." Maria glared at a burned stall. "We can't wait around for him to come and blow up half the city on the off-chance he'll take Tessa Vansant with him. No, we're the damned AET, so we need to handle this. Otherwise, why are we even around?"

Sergeant Weber looked at the ground.

Maria's phone rang. "What?" she snapped without even looking at the caller.

"Your products are ready."

It took her a few seconds to recognize Dannec's voice.

She blinked. "That quickly?"

"When you know the right people things often happen quickly, Lieutenant. And I'm the right people."

"Fine, but I'm in the middle of something."

Dannec sighed. "Yes, I saw. Very unfortunate. All the more reason for you to pick these up quickly."

"How about in a couple hours?"

"Reasonable enough. Just give me a call."

"Okay." Maria ended the call.

Sergeant Weber looked at her. "Who was that?"

"Just something I'm looking into. Don't worry about it."

A few hours later and out of uniform, Maria knocked on the elf's door. Dannec opened it with a smile and gestured her inside.

An ornate wooden chest banded in silver sat in the

middle of his living room. She hadn't seen it the last time she'd been in the apartment.

Maria closed the door behind her. "Thanks for getting this handled so quickly. You were right, we have a witch to take down."

The elf patted the chest. "I have everything you need, but there's just the matter of payment."

The AET lieutenant pulled out her phone. "Just give me an account number for your business."

Dannec shook his head and sighed. "We need to be more circumspect about this, don't you think? It's not exactly like I'm a licensed business, Lieutenant."

"Fuck." Maria looked down at the ground, frowning.

The elf was right. She'd never gone so far off the reservation as to need a non-official payment channel. She knew a few tricks to redirect the money, but not enough. Maybe some sort of cryptocurrency might work.

Dannec smiled. "Might I offer a suggestion?"

"What?"

"I don't deal with him directly, but I know of more than a few people who trade goods and services with James Brownstone. He's more than experienced at offering... indirect payments. I'm sure you could route some sort of bonuses to his account that wouldn't attract too much attention, and he could then make sure I receive appropriate payment."

Maria's mind jumped first to the chance of grabbing Brownstone on some sort of money laundering charge before realizing the utter absurdity of trying to prove it while she was trying to circumvent the system herself.

Working with the Devil? I hope Tyler never hears about this.

Hell, I'll go drink in his bar and tell him my sorrows. Maybe he has a better idea.

"I'll figure something out, but I need this shit."

"Fine." The elf stared at her for a moment as if he could read her thoughts. "I trust you, Lieutenant. I know you're good for it."

"You do?"

"Let's just say I trust you'll realize that double-crossing me isn't a good idea for either of us. Plus, it won't do me much good if the ones I'm selling my product to die before they can pay me because I didn't trust them." Dannec ran his hand along the silver band and uttered something in a language she didn't understand. The chest's lid clicked as if a lock inside had opened.

"A passphrase," Dannec explained. He threw open the lid.

"What the fuck?"

Even though she was staring right into it, it was hard to wrap her mind around the fact that a ladder extended into the chest. From what she could see, it looked a good eighteen or so feet wide and ten feet deep, even if it only looked about a couple feet long and a foot high on the outside.

Dannec stepped onto the ladder and climbed into the chest. From the bottom, he waved Maria in. She hesitated for a moment before following. There were several small tables inside which contained a variety of artifacts. Anti-magic deflector necklaces sat on one in a pile. The shape of the crystals was different than it had been on the deflectors they'd purchased before, but they otherwise didn't look that different.

The elf nodded at the table. "As you can see, Lieutenant, I have everything you need."

"Yeah, you do, and you're going to get a lot of money from me soon."

"And a favor."

"Yeah, a favor." Maria shook her head. "Why do I feel like I might be making a mistake?"

"There are no mistakes in life, Lieutenant, only under-exploited opportunities."

Trey yawned and stretched and hopped out of bed. He grabbed a robe from the floor and lightly slapped his face. "Shit, didn't mean to sleep so long."

It'd been a busy few days, and he'd ended up more tired than he'd realized. Between his aunt, bounties, and James, it was hard not to be exhausted.

Whining wouldn't change anything, though. James wasn't going to wait around and do nothing, so Trey couldn't either. Every bounty Trey pulled off the streets meant money and enhanced the rep of the Brownstone Agency. No man could complain about earning more money.

Got to show my aunt the kind of man I am now.

Before leaving the bedroom of the Airbnb rental, Trey grabbed his phone. He could eat and look for possible bounties at the same time. There were a few things in the fridge they'd picked up, but he'd need a decent meal if he were going to function that day.

"Hey, Auntie Charlyce, did you want to go somewhere

for breakfast?" he called. "Or did you want an hour or two?"

His stomach rumbled as he waited for her response.

"Auntie Charlyce? You hear me?"

Trey frowned and walked over to her room. The door was open.

He peeked inside. Her room was empty.

There were only two bathrooms in the rental, the en-suite connected to his bedroom and a larger main bathroom. He walked to the other bathroom. The door was open, and his aunt wasn't there.

Where the fuck is she? I don't have time for hide and seek.

"Shit." Trey took a few deep breaths and checked every other room in the one-story house. Unless his aunt had suddenly learned invisibility magic, she was gone, and she hadn't left a note.

Damn it! I thought she was legit about changing, but maybe she couldn't handle it. Maybe the idea that she'd actually have to work pushed her back onto the street.

Trey stared down at his phone and pondered calling her.

Someone knocked on his door.

Trey's gaze darted to his room. He'd left his guns there.

"Nah, I shouldn't be that paranoid. I haven't taken down anyone who's gonna go through the trouble to track my ass down, at least not until they get out of prison." He headed to the door and opened it, expecting some asshole trying to get him to switch pest-control services.

The joke was on them. It wasn't even his house.

His aunt stood on the other side with a small bag of donuts and a drink carrier holding two cups of coffee.

Trey blinked, confusion swallowing his surprise. His aunt stepped past him and headed into the dining room to deposit the goodies on the table.

"Where you been?" Trey inquired.

"I wanted to check on Dina so I took a bus to the CPS office, but they wouldn't let me see her."

Trey shrugged. "Not a big surprise. You're not a relative. To them, you're just some homeless woman."

"Yeah, I guess so. When I was getting off the bus I saw a donut place, so I figured I'd grab a few." She laughed. "I used up the last little bit of money I had, so I need a new job. I'm ready to clock in on time."

"Good to hear." Trey and his aunt sat at the dining room table. He brought up the bounty hunting app and spun the phone so she could see it. "This is what we go off most of the time. There's a city-specific app for LA, too."

Aunt Charlyce laughed. "It's like you're shopping online for criminals."

"Pretty much. I'm a level-three bounty hunter because I've brought in at least one level-three bounty. I'm licensed and insured and all that, but if I get my ass killed by a level five our insurance company might not pay out."

"Those are magical folks, mostly, aren't they?"

"Some terrorist leaders and cartel types can get a little higher, but yeah. You go above three, it's almost always some guy with magic. The specific rules depend on the place issuing the bounty, so it varies from state to state." He snorted. "Politicians got to even make stopping criminals hard."

His aunt clucked her tongue. "You shouldn't be going after strange magical folks anyway."

"Not yet anyway." Trey grinned. "Who knows about the future? For now, though, I'm trying to focus mostly on level one and two guys. I can handle those fools easy. A lot of low-level guys aren't even that dangerous. They have bounties on them because of their crimes and they're good at hiding, but they aren't that dangerous. But if a guy's level two, it usually means the asshole at least knows his way around a gun or knife. Not always, though."

He picked up his coffee and opened the donut box to grab a maple bar. His aunt snatched a donut of her own. Neither spoke for a few moments as they nibbled on their food and sipped their coffees.

Aunt Charlyce finished her donut and sighed. "This job of yours is dangerous, but at the same time, I can't help but be proud of you. You're making money, and helping keep the cities safer."

"Thanks." He watched her for a moment. "There's just one thing I still need to ask you about before we go find some asshole to drag into the police."

"What?"

"Do you want me to tell Nana you're back? I didn't want to say anything to her until I knew for sure."

Aunt Charlyce stared down at her hands and shook her head. "Not yet, Trey. Maybe when I know we've got this."

"Fair enough. For now, I'm just happy to have more family. Now, let's go shopping for a criminal."

James stared into the mirror, trying to resist the urge to slam his fist into it. He'd thought Peyton sending him to

Tim meant he'd find Red Eyes in one night. The plan was to end the threat in one quick fight. Everyone would be safer, and Dina's father would have been avenged.

No other bodies had been found since the dead bounty hunter, but that provided little comfort. Red Eyes was speeding up and expanding his targets overall. The fact that he'd killed Lance proved that. The bastard could have run, but he hadn't.

Even worse, a class-four bounty hunter was better equipped to take on a threat like Red Eyes than your average cop. If James didn't stop the killer soon, the bastard would grow cocky and start picking off people left and right. The streets of Las Vegas would run with blood.

"Fucking asshole," he rumbled. "Why don't you just come out and fight? Why all the hide and seek? You know I'm gonna kick your ass. Is that it?"

The bounty hunter's heart thundered, and he half-considered looking up some level-three bounties so he could work off some of his frustration.

"Fucking Red Eyes."

James took several deep breaths and marched over to his phone, which was on the nightstand. He needed some-thing to ground him. He picked up the phone and called Alison.

The phone kept ringing and he glanced at the time.

Shit, it's still early morning. She's probably in magical broom-making class or some shit.

"Hey, Dad," she answered.

James let out a grunt by way of a response.

Alison laughed. "Very articulate."

"Just wanted to check on you."

"Why?"

"Uh, 'cause you're my daughter?" James sighed. Hearing her voice slowed his heart rate, and she wasn't close enough to sense his reasons for calling.

Wonder what color embarrassment is?

Alison laughed. "Yeah, overprotective much? I'm sorry, Dad. I'd love to talk, but I'm between classes, so I don't have a lot of time. You can call me later if you want."

"Nah, that's okay. Just checking in, is all."

"Okay, talk to you later. Love you."

"Love you."

The teen ended the call.

James took a few deep breaths. The call had centered him, and now he could go back to thinking about the best way to track down Red Eyes.

He'd been thinking the question over for a few minutes when his phone chimed with a text from Alison.

I'm fine, Dad. Nothing is going on here that you need to worry about. Don't bring work home. And if someone annoys me, I'll just put my size-six Alison Brownstones up their ass. Love, Me.

James chuckled. "Don't bring work home, huh?" He glanced around the hotel room. "Not at home, but I guess you can tell even when I'm thousands of miles away."

Calling his daughter, legal or otherwise, might have been a good way to calm his fiery blood, but it didn't inspire any new ideas for tracking the killer. He did know another woman who knew more than a few things about tracking people and beating them down.

James blasted off a text to Shay and waited. He had no

idea with the time zones if she'd even be awake, but it was worth a shot. His phone rang a couple of minutes later.

"Hey, Shay."

"Having some trouble, huh? What's the problem? The minute I leave the country you fall to pieces and sob until I return?

James snorted. "Normally, I wouldn't give a shit about it taking a day or two to find the fucker, but this guy needs to go down before he hurts more innocent people."

"You're missing the obvious."

"Huh? How do you know? You're not even here."

Shay scoffed. "Magical support, Oh Mighty Bounty Hunter."

"I don't need magic to kill this guy. I just need to be there to pound his fucking head into the ground until he stops moving."

"You bitched to me about not being able to find him in your text. That's what I'm talking about. Get some sort of magical tracking help. I doubt this asshole has a bunch of anti-tracking magic on him."

"I shouldn't use shit I don't understand. It's bad to get reliant on that kind of crap."

Shay barked out a harsh laugh. "Are you fucking serious? For fuck's sake, you've got nothing now, so what will you lose if you try? The worst that will happen is you get nothing, or, you know, maybe you actually track down the fucker so you can do what you're aching to do. Or you can sit there and whine about how you don't like magic. Your choice."

James grumbled under his breath. "Well, maybe I'll look

into it. Not saying I'll use it, but you've got a point. It's not like I've got anything to lose."

"Glad to see you can buy a clue every now and again."

He took a deep breath. "Thanks. Everything okay with you?"

Shay snickered. "Nothing I can't handle, but I do have some stuff I have to take care of soon."

"It's fine. I think I should call around and see if I can find someone to help me out with some magic. Even if it's gonna end up being fucking complicated, you're right—I should use it."

"Life's not simple, James. At some point, you're just gonna have to accept that."

He grunted. "Don't I know it."

"Don't die, or if you do die, make sure it's not some cheap way. Talk to you later."

James chuckled. "Sure."

Shay hung up, and the bounty hunter immediately dialed Zoe.

You're making my life complicated, Shay. Still willing to pay the price, though.

Four rings passed before the potions witch picked up.

A huge yawn came over the line. "James? Why are you calling me so early? You know how I love to sleep in."

"I think that's called sleeping off a hangover, Zoe."

She tittered. "True, but still—I thought we had an understanding."

"Yeah, we did. Sorry to bother you, but I'm hunting some fucked-up serial killer in Las Vegas and I thought maybe you'd know someone who could help me out with a little magical tracking."

"Oh. I see. Hrmm. I do know…someone who might be able to help you out, but she's a bit odd."

"Says the always-drunk witch."

"We all have our ways of doing magic, James." She gulped down something on the other end.

Huh. You're bitching about me waking you up, but you're already pounding booze?

"This is important. If she can help me, I can probably stop a crazed killer."

Zoe sighed. "Okay, okay. Her name is Margarete. You can find her in the shark tank at the Golden Nugget."

"You mean near the tank?"

"I mean *in* the tank."

James blinked. "Huh, that's different."

"Like I said, odd. Be prepared, James. This woman won't just want money. She won't harm you, I guarantee that, but still, keep your wits about you."

"She's just some water witch or something, right? How bad could she be?"

"You'll see."

19

Maria walked into the Black Sun. They weren't officially open yet, so Tyler and Kathy were still pulling chairs down and wiping tables.

Tyler looked up from his table near the front. "Lieutenant Hall! What are you doing here so early?"

She nodded toward the back. "I want to talk to you about something in private."

The bartender nodded and set his rag down. He navigated through the tables with the cop behind him until they reached the back hallway and his office.

Tyler settled behind his desk, but Maria remained standing after closing the door.

She pointed with her thumb toward the door. "How nice to see you doing honest work."

The bartender chuckled. "At least the public freely pays me for a service. I'm not relying on taxes for my salary."

"Whatever. People want the police."

"Which is why you're paid so well?"

Maria rolled her eyes. "You sell booze. It's hard not to

make money when you're selling booze, but somehow you were having trouble until recently."

Tyler winced. "Ouch."

The AET lieutenant dropped into a chair. "Look, I need to talk to you about something money-related anyway."

"Sandwich and chips costs what it says on the menu above the bar." He leaned forward. "But the price of information is negotiable."

Maria took a deep breath. Asking a criminal to effectively help her divert money to someone who was probably another criminal blew past all sorts of lines, but she wasn't doing any of this to get rich. She was just trying to make sure her men didn't get hurt when they next had to fight a dangerous enhanced threat.

Fuck it. If I go down for saving cop's lives, I don't give a shit.

"I've sourced some...magical supplies from an Oriceran."

"You mean the guy I sent you to?" Tyler smirked.

Maria nodded. "Yeah. I need to get him money, but it's not like I can just electronically transfer it from the normal police accounts." She shrugged. "Government runs on paperwork, and this guy's not a real big fan."

Tyler steepled his fingers. "Makes sense. You don't have some sort of special slush fund for undercover shit or something you could use?"

"The department, sure. AET? We don't do undercover work. Besides, I'm getting the feeling this guy's going to want something more direct. I need a third party both sides can use." She snorted. "The guy actually suggested Brownstone."

Tyler frowned. "Fuck that. You want Brownstone

knowing about your secret supply chains? Once he knows about that shit, you'll never be able to go against him."

"Exactly. I need someone else, and I was wondering if you had any ideas."

The man leaned back in his chair with a grin. "Yeah, I've got a great idea."

"Well, spill it."

He pointed to his head. "What about me?"

"Huh? You?"

Tyler nodded. "Yeah. Dannec knows me. You know me. You know I'm not going to fuck you over because you help maintain the neutrality of the Black Sun."

Maria narrowed her eyes. "I doubt you're going to do this out of the goodness of your heart."

"No, but I will for one percent, which is a pretty damn good deal, I'd say, all things considered."

The lieutenant thought the idea over. By enforcing neutrality at the Black Sun she'd long ago crossed the line of helping out a criminal, and if she could get the criminal's help in protecting AET officers from maniacs like Tessa Vansant, a little profit for the man didn't seem so out of line. At least Tyler wasn't going to rampage through a farmer's market murdering twelve people on a whim.

Maria nodded. "I think this might work."

"I'll go ahead and contact Dannec about the first ten percent. It'll take me about a week to get a legit cover business set up so I can handle the other ninety."

"Huh."

"What is it?"

Maria stood. "Just thinking about how you know my business, too."

Tyler shrugged. "I'm many things, but I'm not an enhanced threat, and besides, if I fuck you over the cops stop enforcing the neutrality of this place. Trust me. I'm making a lot more money than I ever did before because people know they can come here without trouble and talk with all sorts of...interesting people."

"Just keep that in mind if you ever decide to try, Tyler." Maria turned to leave. "Otherwise, we'll have more trouble like that shit that went down when Brownstone tricked those assholes into coming here. Glad to see how quickly you got everything cleaned up from his practical joke." She shrugged. "Assuming it was him. We can't prove it."

Tyler shot out his chair. "Oh, it was that fucker, all right. I know it was. He thought it was so fucking funny to get a bunch of assholes to shoot up my bar. Fucking cocky piece of shit. I hope he chokes on a complimentary steak in Vegas."

Maria laughed. The chief might have told her to shut the hell up about Brownstone, but it was nice to know there was always one place she could go and bitch about him.

Bringing cops and crooks together. You're a special breed of asshole, Brownstone.

James imagined that if he were sent to hell, it'd probably look like a casino. Too many fucking people, too many fucking flashing lights, everything just complicated. Casinos were the fucking high temples of complication.

Gambling itself was complicated, and based around the

stupidest principle in the world: that a person could get something for nothing. He walked through the casino until he reached the pool area.

Low white chairs surrounded the swimming pool, which had a massive tank filled with small sharks in the center. Various clear water slide tubes ran through the tank. Someone might not be able to swim with the sharks, but they could at least slide past them. Not James' idea of fun, but he could see how someone might like it.

Huh. Wonder what it'd be like to get in a fight with a shark?

No one paid the bounty hunter much attention as they splashed in the pool or wandered to and from the outdoor bar.

I'm supposed to find someone in the pool, then? Is that what Zoe meant? She couldn't seriously mean the witch would be in the shark tank.

James searched the area for anyone who looked like a witch, but a casino resort pool filled with drunken tourists in swimsuits wasn't exactly lacking odd or exotic women.

"You're looking for someone," commented a sultry voice from behind.

James turned to find a beautiful and slender young woman in a metallic green bikini standing behind him. Given that only her legs were wet, she must have been only wading.

His neck tensed. Something about her was slightly off, but he couldn't quite place it. Something about the look in her eyes... Her body and face suggested she was in her early twenties, but something in her eyes spoke of someone or something far more ancient.

"You're looking for me, aren't you, Mr. Brownstone?" The woman offered him a dazzling white smile.

"Who are you?" The last thing he wanted to do was assume anything.

"Margarete. A mutual friend let me know you might be coming."

The tension drained away from his neck and stomach. He nodded toward the pool. "I thought you'd be a witch, but what…you're some kind of mermaid or some shit like that?"

Margarete smiled and shrugged, ignoring the question. "What did you need?"

James thought about pressing her for her true identity, but he wasn't there to do a census of strange magical beings. He was there to get magical help.

"I need to find a man."

"Honey, don't we all?"

James' face twitched.

Margarete laughed. "Oh, you're looking rather stiff. Maybe you need to dip something hard somewhere soft. Several times." She winked.

He groaned. "It still takes me a while to get a lot of her shit when she says it, but you sound like Shay."

"Oh? Sounds like my type of girl."

James stared at the woman. "You like to kill?"

Margarete let out a throaty laugh. "Not my first choice, or even my second. How can I ride them all night long if they are dead?"

No, not Shay. This woman was Zoe before she'd decided James was too dangerous to flirt with.

Yeah, no wonder you two are friends.

James opened his mouth and then shut it. His discussion with Margarete had taken all his focus; he hadn't even noticed he couldn't hear any other sounds. The mouths of the scores of people around them moved and people splashed in the pool, but none of the noise reached his ears.

"Guess we can talk about business here without being overheard?"

Margarete nodded. "For the moment."

"I'm hunting the Red Eyes Killer. Tech and the cops aren't finding him and pushing street contacts isn't helping. I'm looking for some magical tracking, and I was told you could help."

"I can. For a price."

James shrugged. "I know you don't want cash, so what do you want?"

Margarete tilted her head and gave him a seductive smile. "I know what I *really* want, but I also can tell by looking at you that you won't give it to me."

James decided that some questions were better left unasked. "Uh, what else, then?"

"I want a memory."

"Huh?"

"A memory. Nothing special. I'll take your memory of eating breakfast this morning."

James grunted. "Are you fucking kidding me?"

Margarete shook her head. "It's not something you need, is it?"

"This shit is weird. Why does magic have to be so fucking complicated?"

The smile finally vanished from the woman's face. "If it

were any easier, even people like you wouldn't be able to push back the darkness, James Brownstone."

The statement hung in the air for a long moment before James cleared his throat. "You seriously want my memory of eating a Double-Double and fries at In-N-Out for payment?" James shook his head, not believing what he was hearing. This shit was weird even for magic.

The redhead nodded. "Yes. That'll do nicely."

"And what are you going to do with my memory?"

"Experience one moment of simple joy as James Brownstone."

He couldn't argue too much with that. Double-Doubles were damned good. Not Jessie Rae's, but they still hit the spot.

James rubbed the back of his neck. He didn't trust the woman, but Zoe wouldn't recommend someone who was going to fuck with him too badly.

He sucked in a breath. "Just need to give you my memory?"

"Yeah, it'll be gone, and you won't remember what you had."

James shrugged. "Sure, why the fuck not?"

Margarete grinned and half-closed her eyes.

The bounty hunter's body tingled for a moment, and his head throbbed slightly. "What the fuck are you doing?"

"Just taking my payment." Margarete leaned forward. "Tell me, James, what did you have for breakfast this morning."

"I... Shit, I can't remember." He blinked several times. "I can't even remember where." He narrowed his eyes. "I thought you were going to just take my memory of what I ate."

"Consider it a lesson, James. It's hard to yank a single thread without causing ripples." She shrugged.

His memory had always been a blessing and a curse. The idea of simply forgetting something so banal it tightened his stomach and neck. It was an odd experience, and he wasn't sure if it was exhilarating or annoying as fuck. He also wasn't sure if the woman had screwed him over in some way he wouldn't realize for a long time.

Margarete's face broke into a broad grin. "Ah, yes, that was what I wanted. *That* sensation." She inhaled and slowly breathed out. "I'll track down your killer for you, but I need a focus."

James stared at her for a moment, still considering interrogating her about what the hell had just happened.

Whatever. If this mermaid or witch or whatever the hell she is fucked me over, it's already too late. I need to get Red Eyes. I can always come back for her some other time.

"What's a focus?" James inquired.

"In this case, something physically connected to them. A finger or toe would be nice." She laughed. "But a hair will do; anything connected to their body."

"Does it have to be as big as a hair?"

She shook her head. "No, a small particle really."

"Like a DNA sample?"

"I suppose."

James nodded. "Okay, I'll get it for you."

"Then I'll get you your killer."

Trey and his aunt pulled up to the curb of a huge condo building a few blocks off Las Vegas Boulevard. Their target for the day was only a level one, but she specialized in financial fraud, particularly of the elderly, so it'd be sweet as hell to take her down.

The bounty hunter chuckled. "When I'm trying to be slick I just use the delivery strategy—you know, walk up with a pizza box or something like that—but if that doesn't work, I'll just kick the door in." He jerked his thumb toward the backseat. "That's why I have the empty pizza boxes back there, and a few bags from delivery places."

Aunt Charlyce tsked. "So if you can't trick 'em you just bust down their door?"

"Yep." Trey threw open his door and stepped out of the truck. "Haven't lost a bounty yet."

His aunt stepped out and fell in behind him as they made their way to the lobby and then down a hallway to their target: Unit Three. His aunt grabbed his arm and shook her head as they approached the door.

"You don't even have a pizza box," she pointed out.

Trey tugged at his suit. "Maybe I'll claim I'm with the census or some shit like that."

Aunt Charlyce sighed and held up a finger. "Wait here. Watch and learn, little one."

Trey scoffed. "Little one? Okay, show me what you've got." He crossed his arms and waited.

His aunt disappeared down the hallway.

What the fuck is she playing at?

Aunt Charlyce remerged a minute later pushing a laden cleaning cart down the hallway.

Trey eyed the cart. "What's the deal?"

"It's like I told Mr. Brownstone—no one wants to notice the homeless. Background noise." She winked. "Same with the help. No one sees anything but the tools. It's not like a delivery man. Everybody notices the delivery man."

Trey gave her an appreciative nod. He'd thought a few fake pizza boxes was being clever, but in truth, he relished the idea of kicking in a bounty's door and yelling for them to surrender. A different kind of Trojan Horse action could help them take the bounty completely off-guard.

He nodded. "I'll be around the corner." He jogged down to the end of the hallway and tugged out his gun.

His aunt pushed the cart into clear view of the camera over the door and knocked.

"What?" snapped a severe female voice over the intercom.

Trey's aunt smiled up at the camera. "Excuse me, miss. I'm terribly sorry to be bothering you, but I need to put in some anti-smell pucks in your bathroom and kitchen."

"I didn't ask for any of that."

"I know, miss. I'm super sorry. It's got nothing to do with you. It's preventative. The unit next door, well, I can't reveal all the details, but there's an issue, and we're worried the smell's gonna spread to your place."

"Damn it," the woman growled over the intercom. "It's those damned Indians in four. Why the hell can't they cook their food at the restaurant like all the rest of them? One second." The door clicked open and a scowling woman in a suit stepped out. "Just make it quick. I'm in the middle of something."

Aunt Charlyce smiled and pushed the cart halfway in and stopped when it fully blocked the door.

Trey darted around the corner, his gun at the ready. "Brownstone Agency here to take your level-one ass in." He kept his gun trained on the bounty. "Now, please don't make me get violent. You won't like me when I get violent."

The woman glared at Trey. For a second she looked like she wanted to run, but instead, she turned and raised her hands above her head. Trey quickly cuffed her.

"This is ridiculous," the bounty snarled. "I'm not some common criminal."

Trey pushed her down the hall. "Nah, you definitely ain't that. If you were, you wouldn't have a bounty."

"All I did was make a little money. It wasn't a *real* crime."

Aunt Charlyce snorted. "You tricked money out of little old ladies."

"Every prospectus I sent out to potential clients encouraged them to do their due diligence. It's not my fault they didn't listen."

Trey snorted. "Were you just born a bitch, or did you have to take special pills for it?"

"I'm just saying that if people get tricked, it's their own fault."

Aunt Charlyce laughed. "So it's your own fault that we tricked you into opening the door?"

The woman harrumphed, clearly entranced by her own carefully curated sense of superiority. Trey continued guiding the bounty down the hall. He sighed and shook his head.

At the other end of the hallway, a middle-aged Indian

woman opened her door and stuck her head out, curious about all the commotion.

The bounty grimaced. "Your food! It's *your* food that's fucking with my life!"

Trey and his aunt laughed.

20

James' chair creaked underneath his heavy frame as he waited to talk to Detective West or his partner. He'd thought they'd be eager to see him, but the way the desk sergeant kept eyeing him, the bounty hunter was convinced that the police would have preferred him anywhere but there. Maybe it was just because of the way everyone kept focusing on him.

Guess that's the price of being famous.

He'd just pulled out his phone to check on the latest barbeque news when Detective West stepped around the corner.

"Mr. Brownstone, please come with me." The detective turned without even waiting.

James stood and followed him down the hallway into a small interrogation room. Detective Lafayette already sat inside at a plain white table.

Detective West closed the door behind James once they were both inside the room. "Your message mentioned that you needed something?"

"Yeah. A DNA sample."

The two cops exchanged glances and Detective West sighed. "I...don't think that's possible."

"Huh? You gave me a bunch of evidence before."

The cop shook his head. "I let you know a few things we found, and even that was stretching things. I'm not sure giving you DNA will be okay. We don't want to fuck up the case."

"You want this guy or not? If you give me DNA, I can track his ass down. The clock's ticking, and you're only lucky that he hasn't killed anyone else." He frowned. "Or he has, and you just haven't found the bodies yet."

The cops' faces tightened. They looked at each other again, and Detective Lafayette nodded to his partner.

"Wait here, Brownstone," Detective West ordered. "I'll see what I can do."

He disappeared into the hallway, and James pulled out his phone to read up on a few new experimental barbeque spice blends. His annoyance made him want to chat even less than usual.

He wanted to nail Red Eyes as soon as possible, but he needed the cops' cooperation to do that. Otherwise, it was back to hitting street contacts and being too late to stop murders. James had made a promise to that little girl, and he intended to keep it.

After a few minutes, Detective Lafayette cleared his throat. "Hey, Brownstone. "I'm curious about something."

James looked up from his phone. "What?"

"Why do you do it?"

"Do what?"

"Bounty hunting. You're a tough guy. You could have

gotten involved in some sort of enhanced MMA league or some shit like that. Fuck, you could have been a criminal."

James snorted. "You think everyone who is tough is a criminal?"

"I've been a cop a long time, and I think a lot of people get drunk on power, magical or otherwise."

The bounty hunter stared at the cop. Maybe it was the nature of the case or maybe it was because Shay was out of the country, but for some reason, the truth spilled from his lips before he could stop it.

"Revenge," James rumbled.

"Revenge?"

"Or justice—whatever the fuck you want to call it. The truth is, I'm an orphan." No reason for the police officer to know he was an *alien* orphan. "I ended up in a Catholic orphanage. I don't remember my real parents, but there was a priest who took me under his wing, and he died protecting me." James' hand curled into a fist "That lit a fire in me. I...don't know any other way to burn off the injustice."

An odd expression settled over the cop's face and he nodded.

"What?" James barked.

"Just...surprised, I guess. Everyone knows you're tough, and you've got a good reputation for helping cops, but I still thought that in the end, you were in it for the money. But I don't get it. If your job is more about justice than money, why not become a cop?"

James shook his head. "I don't play well by other people's rules, and I like my life simple. Being a cop is all about too many complicated fucking rules."

Detective Lafayette chuckled. "Damn, don't I know it!"

Detective West reentered the room holding a small plastic bag with a vial inside.

"We're putting our asses on the line here, Brownstone, so we'll need to go with you."

James grunted. "Does that fuck with my bounty income?"

"You can have your bounty." The detective shrugged. "But you were the guy saying this wasn't about the money."

"Doesn't mean I don't still want to try to make some money, and if I have to put Red Eyes down to stop him, I'm not gonna shy away from it."

The detective shrugged. "Not complaining."

Sergeant Weber threw open the door to Maria's office, his breathing hard and his face red.

"What the fuck happened to you?" Maria demanded.

"We just got a tip on Tessa Vansant."

"And?"

"A woman matching her description was asking about a tour visit by Nadina. The event's in two days at a country club."

"Who the fuck is Nadina?"

Sergeant Weber stared at her like she was an idiot. She wanted to punch him for that. "The elf?"

"I don't know the name of every fucking elf in Los Angeles, Weber."

He shrugged. "She won *Barbeque Wars: The Next Genera-*

tion. She's kind of famous now—an elf doing barbeque and all that."

"Oh, so some reality-show chick with pointy ears. Got it."

Weber looked like he wanted to complain about the characterization but kept his mouth shut.

Maria rubbed her chin. "So we don't know where Tessa is, but we might know where she'll be."

"Yeah."

"And the source of the tip?"

"Anonymous male over the phone. We couldn't trace it. From what IT tells me, whoever it was made sure we wouldn't be able to."

Is that you showing a tiny slice of conscience, Tyler? I'll do us both a favor and not ask you about it. Then again, maybe it's not you.

Maria frowned, wondering about a few other possibilities. "That's fucking suspicious."

"Yeah, but this is also the only lead we have."

"We might be being set up." Maria shook her head. "What the fuck ever. We should contact the country club. They need to cancel the event."

"Huh? I thought you would have wanted us to ambush Vansant."

Maria shrugged. "I'm not going to use a bunch of civilians as bait. Protect and serve." She grinned. "Or maybe we *shouldn't* cancel it."

Weber blinked. "I'm even more confused. You're contradicting yourself."

The lieutenant grabbed a jacket off the hook on her door. "We can use civilians as bait, as long as they aren't actually there. Contact the country club. We'll just station cops there as fake guests or something, so no one has to be at risk." She slipped on the coat.

"Why do you need the coat? It's been hot for a while."

"Don't worry about me, Weber, just contact the country club. I'm going to look into another avenue for tracking this bitch's ass down."

Maria drove to Dannec's apartment building still in uniform, but in her personal car. She threw the jacket on and zipped it up. Her uniform pants were still visible, but without the rest of the uniform obvious she didn't scream cop—or at least her clothes didn't.

She made her way to his door, and her jaw dropped when she reached his apartment—or where his apartment should have been. There was no door there anymore, just a wall.

"You've got to be fucking kidding me," Maria growled. She kicked the wall and walked away.

Well, at least the fucker gave me the deflectors before he tele-ported his apartment back to Oriceran or wherever.

Maria stomped all the way back to her car and slipped into the driver's seat, then took a few deep breaths. There were too many damn variables in play. The tip about Tessa Vansant might be a trap, or it might be a legit lead. Two days wasn't a lot of time to set up a sting, and that was assuming the country club agreed.

If the police made too much noise, they might spook

her. Tessa might go somewhere else to butcher innocent people. The woman needed to be stopped and soon.

I'm going to protect and serve my city by putting that bitch in the ground.

Maria pulled off her jacket and tossed it on the passenger seat, where stray rays of sunlight glinted off her badge. She stared down at the metal and frowned.

"Maybe Tyler wasn't just talking about people not trusting cops when he told me not to dress in my uniform."

Maria removed her uniform top and stepped out of the car. She looked strange in only her white undershirt, uniform pants, and polished boots, but she didn't give a shit about looking weird if it worked.

The AET lieutenant marched back to Dannec's apartment, and this time the door was there.

"Fucking magic. Why does it have to be so obnoxious?"

She knocked on the door, and it opened.

Dannec stood on the other side with a sly smile on his face as if he knew what she'd been through.

Fucker. I'm only not saying shit because you're helping me.

He motioned her inside, and Maria entered.

"I wasn't expecting you again so soon, Lieutenant."

"If you can get me deflectors, you can probably get quick access to tracking magic, right? Or could help me track a suspect?"

Dannec gave a slight shrug. "Maybe. If I had some sort of physical sample from the target I could help you, but it's my understanding that there are legal barriers to using that sort of thing. You're required to be able to track a suspect down with non-magical means, I believe. Any tracking magic I could give you would taint your investigation, and you wouldn't get a conviction."

Maria snorted. "I want to find them, not convict them."

The corners of Dannec's mouth turned up. "Oh. In that case, I might be able to get something for you."

The ass-kicking the team had received from Brownstone's floozy still weighed heavily on the lieutenant's mind. LAPD AET was one of the best equipped in the country. She'd thought they were prepared for anything with all their weapons and gear, but the encounter had proved they weren't. They had been damned lucky that none of the officers had been killed.

She needed better support this time. She needed to make sure her men went home and not to the coroner's office at the end of the day.

Maria sighed and shook her head. She was already bending so many rules.

I'll be fucking Brownstone before this is all over, doing whatever the hell I please because the ends justify the means. Fuck. I need to rein this shit in at least some.

She stared down at her hands and shook her head. "Never mind, Dannec."

Genuine surprise crossed the elf's face. "Never mind?"

"I'm already in with you pretty deeply and I do have a lead, so I'm going to play this like a cop, not like some witch. But thanks for seeing me."

"Very well, Lieutenant Hall. You always know where to find me if you need me."

Maria turned toward the door.

"One last thing," the elf called. "Our mutual friend contacted me. I'm happy with your payment efforts so far."

"Glad you're happy. Thanks for the deflectors." Maria pushed out of the apartment.

No, I'm not fucking Brownstone, not yet. We'll catch Tessa the old-fashioned way.

James led the detectives to the pool and shark tank but stopped about forty feet away.

"You wait here."

Detective West frowned. "Why?"

"Because I don't know if my contact is okay with cops."

The cops nodded.

James continued toward the pool and Margarete appeared out of nowhere a few seconds later. He frowned. He'd been looking straight ahead, and she hadn't been there, but now she stood in front of him as if she'd been there for an hour.

This time she wasn't in a green bikini, but a tight metallic green dress that accentuated her curves and contrasted with her red hair. She wasn't wearing any shoes, and water clung to the bottom of her legs.

"Damn," Detective West murmured. "That's his contact? She looks fucking hot. Like surface-of-the-sun hot. How does Brownstone not roll over for her? Maybe he's gay?"

James snorted.

Detective Lafayette laughed. "I don't know. I'm half-wondering if I should switch back to Team Hetero and ask her out."

James rolled his eyes and glanced over his shoulder. The cops were a good distance away and weren't yelling, but he could hear them like they were standing right next to him.

"Manipulating sound is easy," Margarete explained as if reading his thoughts. "I was just curious what your friends might be saying. Police officers, I presume."

The bounty hunter nodded. "Yeah. I didn't want them over here until I got your permission."

The woman offered him a flirtatious smile. "Oh, I've no problem with the police. I do enjoy staying on the right side of the law." She waved to the cops and motioned for them to come over.

The detectives hurried to the pair.

Margarete smiled at them both. "Please give me the sample." Detective West reached into his pocket and pulled out the bag holding the vial. He retrieved the vial from the bag and handed it to the redhead.

She took it with a wink. "I already went through the trouble of preparing everything, so this won't take long." She placed the vial in her hand, closed her eyes, and hummed an odd tune James didn't recognize. For some reason, it sounded very old to his ears. Her hand glowed with a dull green light for a few seconds before she opened her eyes. "Interesting."

The bounty hunter and cops all looked at each other, but it was James who finally spoke. "Interesting?"

"This is from someone who was a human originally, but they aren't anymore. They've been modified with dark magic, and whoever did it was plenty evil themselves."

Detective West scrubbed his face with a hand. "Perfect. Just what I wanted to deal with."

"You don't have to deal with it," James pointed out. "I'll do it."

Margarete held out her hand. A small glowing green arrow now rested atop the vial. "Think of it as a magical compass. It'll point the right direction and glow brighter the closer you are."

James took the enchanted vial from her hand. "Thanks. And you don't need anything else other than what I already gave you?"

The detectives both shot each other grins.

I didn't fuck her, you idiots.

"Your payment was more than sufficient." Margarete winked at Detective Lafayette. "By the way, if you ever do want to switch teams, I can assure you that I bat for mine."

She sashayed off, and Detective West stared at her as she left with sad puppy-dog eyes.

"That isn't fair," he murmured. "She hits on the gay guy but not the straight one?"

His partner shook his head. "She's something. Maybe she has a bit of a siren song in her."

James grunted. "Whatever. We've got a killer to catch."

"Damn, Brownstone. You don't want to hit that?"

"I've already got a woman, and she's complicated enough."

T rey smiled to himself as he stepped up to the ATM. He'd already made the necessary transfers to the Brownstone Agency account, and now it was time to reward his aunt for her help. The operation had gone smoothly, and he hadn't even needed to get violent.

He didn't mind kicking ass and was proud of his strength, but he wasn't a thug and didn't enjoy hurting people for the sake of it. Especially women, even if they were greedy bitches. Aunt Charlyce's plan had earned him one of his easiest payouts so far as a bounty hunter.

Trey swiped his phone across the ATM pad and waited for the prompts to pop up on the screen. He entered his information and waited as the machine spat out several large-denomination bills.

He made his way back to his F-350 and held out the bills.

Aunt Charlyce shook her head. "I thought we already talked about this. I ain't taking money from you."

"This isn't about charity or family. This is about paying

someone for a job. You're gonna be an administrative assistant, but today you worked as a bounty hunter. I didn't have to beat anyone's ass or shoot anyone because of you. You worked the job with me, including getting the bitch out of her condo without any trouble. You earned this, and I'm not gonna take no for an answer." He locked gazes with her.

She eyed the money for a few long seconds before taking the bills and stuffing them in her pocket. The discomfort on her face disappeared after a few seconds, a warm smile taking its place.

"I know just what to do with it."

After a quick trip to a toy store, Trey drove to the CPS office at his aunt's request. She wanted to meet Dina again. Unlike last time, a few quick calls made it possible.

Trey called James, and the big man happened to already be with the cops. They agreed to call ahead and let the CPS workers know Aunt Charlyce could meet with the girl.

She deserves it. I don't know why she's so set on that girl, but whatever small light helps keep her moving forward is fine by me.

Trey chuckled as he eyed the huge stuffed angel in the backseat. His aunt had been stingy when he was younger, but he understood that the Charlyce sitting next to him now and the woman he had known years ago were very different people.

Give a hand up and not out, and don't focus on the past. Maybe that's the only way anyone can move forward.

From what Trey understood, Dina hadn't been placed in a foster family or in a group home yet only because the police were still concerned about her being targeted by the Red Eyes Killer. The CPS building was close enough to the police station that they didn't need to station any personnel to guard her, but could still intervene if the killer showed up.

If Aunt Charlyce didn't visit her now, there might not be a good chance for her to do it again. He doubted a new foster family would want her hanging around, even if she no longer looked like the homeless woman she'd been for so many years.

They arrived at their destination and Trey parked the truck in front of the building.

"You ready?"

Aunt Charlyce smiled. "More than ready."

They made their way inside to the front desk, his aunt lugging the angel.

Trey adjusted his tie and flashed the receptionist a smile. "I'm Trey Garfield. The police should have called ahead about our visit."

The woman nodded. "Yes, Detective West contacted us about Dina." She stood with a smile. "Just let me show you the way, Mr. Garfield."

She led them down the hallway to the playroom. Another CPS employee stood outside and nodded toward the door.

The woman sighed. "Please try and avoid talking about the incident."

Aunt Charlyce held up the angel. "I just want to give her

this. I want my little angel to feel good and know that there are a lot of people who care about her."

The woman gave a shallow nod, slight discomfort still on her face.

Trey and his aunt stepped inside. He moved to the corner and crossed his arms, just watching quietly. His family was involved so he couldn't say it wasn't his business, but it still felt like it should be a private moment between his aunt and the girl.

Dina sat at a table coloring a picture. Aunt Charlyce set the angel in front of the girl and smiled. "Hey, my little angel. Do you remember me?"

The little girl's eyes widened, and she ran over to hug the woman. "It's you! The nice lady who helped me out of the vent and called the police."

"I told you I'd be nearby." Trey's aunt slid the angel toward the girl. "Here's your angel, honey. Not only is he soft, but he'll also protect you."

The CPS worker frowned behind Aunt Charlyce. Trey resisted the urge to flip her off.

That girl is happy to see my aunt. You better not mess this moment up.

Dina snuggled the toy. "But what about Mr. Brownstone? Isn't he gonna protect everyone?"

Trey grinned. "Mr. Brownstone is going where big angels fear to tread to make sure little angels can sleep well at night. He'll protect everyone, and he'll make sure the bad guys are the ones afraid."

The green arrow grew increasingly bright as the cops and James barreled toward the edge of town in his F-350.

What the fuck? I spent all that time talking to people, and he's nowhere near central Vegas anymore.

"Guess this is what I get for trusting someone who admitted they were high when they made a deal," James grumbled.

"Huh?" Detective West asked. "What are you talking about? Was that redhead high?"

"Who knows? She's a friend of Zoe's. But that's not what I'm talking about."

The detective looked even more confused than before. "Who's Zoe?"

"Don't worry about it. It's not important." James shook his head. "I've been wasting a lot of time in Rancho Charleston, and we're driving away from there, so all the information I had on where the killer was, was wrong."

"Not wrong, Brownstone, just outdated. We thought we had an MO on this guy, but he keeps changing things. Maybe that was part of his plan all along. At least we're heading toward him now."

James grunted. "I wish I had some fucking clue where we were going."

Detective West glanced down at the glowing vial in the cupholder and then up the street. "Actually, I know exactly where we're going."

He looked at his partner and the other cop nodded back.

James spared a glance at the detective as he changed lanes. "Care to share with the rest of the fucking class, guys?"

"We mentioned three guys who died to you."

"Yeah, what about them?"

"We didn't give you all the information about them. They died in a central Vegas warehouse, but they weren't random victims. We traced them to a lab on the edge of town. They worked security at the place, Anders Laboratory. We interviewed the top guy there as well as another scientist, but they stonewalled us. They came off slimy as hell, but we didn't have enough to get a warrant."

"Laboratory? You telling me these fuckers did some sort of magical experiment and made a magical serial killer?" James growled.

The detective shrugged. "Your guess is as good as mine, but you heard what that hot redhead said. And she's magic, right?

"Something like that."

"Then we're talking about evil assholes who are messing around with dark magic and shit. Not exactly the wheelhouse of homicide detectives."

"Don't worry, I've taken down all sorts of magic users and creatures." The bounty hunter's hands tightened around the wheel. "If these guys had security douches going after Red Eyes, that means they knew where he was. They fucking *knew* and could have told the police so you could send AET..." he gritted his teeth, "or me."

"When we interviewed them they had a creepy-ass vibe. It's like they only cared that we were taking up their time. They didn't even seem to care that their guys had been killed. If what that woman said was right they are more evil than the Red Eyes Killer in a way, because they're supposed to be normal humans."

James took a deep breath and slowly let it out. He eased up on the steering wheel.

"Well, the fucking Prodigal Son is returning home, and I doubt he's going there to beg forgiveness if he already sliced up several of their guys."

Detective Lafayette shrugged. "Maybe we could get a warrant based off this tracking? We could argue eventual discovery."

His partner snorted. "Not with the judges around here. We show up smelling of magic and they'll throw everything out."

"No warrant means they have no reason to let us through the gate."

"Guess we're working this off the clock then until we see something with our normal-ass eyes."

James would have preferred that the cops weren't there, but they seemed as interested in taking down Red Eyes as he was. They needed to understand how shit was going to go down, though. He didn't need some Las Vegas AET getting pissed with him when he sent Red Eyes to hell.

Guess it's a good thing I have a backup healing potion in my truck. If I have to take on the lab assholes and Red Eyes, things are gonna get rough without my amulet.

"Look," James rumbled, "when we get there and know what the fuck is happening, we'll make plans. If he's going back to this lab, it's not to swap recipes. There might not even be anybody at the gate to stop us."

Detective West winced. "Those scientists may be assholes, but we can't be sure that *everyone* there is. Maybe we should get some AET over there."

James shook his head. "If AET shows up it might make

things explode. Like I said, let's check the place out and then figure out what the fuck we're gonna do. If you need to call in more cops or AET then, I'm not gonna bitch too much." He stopped at a red light and stared at Detective West. "And just so we're all on the same page, I'm not planning on taking this guy in, cops or no cops."

"Like I said, we're not going to stop you, but you might lose your bounty money."

"Whatever. I've got plenty of money already. The only reason I even fucking came to Las Vegas was for barbeque."

The light turned green, and he accelerated.

An uneasy silence settled over the trio, and the green arrow grew brighter by the minute. They were closing on the enemy, a monster James had targeted at the request of a little girl.

James' thoughts drifted to how much his life had changed since his simple days with Leeroy. Even with Alison, his initial actions hadn't been altruistic. The girl helped him, so he wanted to repay the favor. Now, though, his fist twitched to smash into Red Eyes' face. Everything about the early killings felt as personal to James as the death of his dog.

Once upon a time, this job was just about getting pricks off the street and making some money. Now I have my own angel, and no amount of money is worth more than her. Is that why I'm so amped up about this shit?

"You better hope they kill you before I do, Red Eyes."

Red Eyes chuckled darkly to himself as he stared down at the top of Anders Laboratory from a mountain ledge. After killing the bounty hunter, he'd had an epiphany. Making angels cry satisfied his hungry soul, but to become death he needed more fear. Purer fear. Las Vegas needed to choke on its terror. Only in a sea of true chaos and panic could his victims experience such fear.

Once Death walked every street corner, he'd have his pick of victims and feast on both their fear and DNA. But as strong as he was, he needed a few more tools for his symphony of death, and not the meager rifles strapped over his shoulders. He needed something dangerous without an operator.

He needed living weapons.

Red Eyes laughed. The fools in the lab had no idea he was coming back.

So many twisted projects sat inside the dark little slice of hell calling itself Anders Laboratory. What good was a science project if it were never shared with the world?

You wanted to become gods, but you're just men playing with a fire you don't understand. I will become a god, and I will first punish your arrogance.

Red Eyes leapt off the ledge, cackling.

Detective Lafayette glanced down at the magical tracker. "Maybe they captured him."

"Who?" his partner asked.

"The Red Eyes Killer. We've been assuming he was going back for revenge or something, but maybe they got him? That'd explain why things got quiet after the last killing."

"Doesn't make a difference. If they captured him, then they need to hand him over to us. It doesn't matter if he's a freak. He's a murder suspect and needs to face justice, and the people responsible for creating that freak need to be tried as well. I'm not going to just let them blow this off and dissect him so they can figure out how to make the next one smarter and stronger."

James chuckled. "And what will you do if they refuse to turn him over or claim he's not there?"

"I guess we'll just have to look the other way while a private citizen makes a ruckus."

"Works for me. All I care about is taking down the Red

Eyes Killer. The rest of this shit with this lab you guys can figure out. That's cop work, not bounty-hunter work."

"Fair enough, Brownstone."

The bounty hunter's phone announced a call from Shay. Normally, he would have put it on speaker, but he didn't want the detectives overhearing anything embarrassing she might say. If he told her she was on speaker, she'd probably purposely try to embarrass him.

James grimaced at the thought as he lifted the phone to this ear. "Hey," he answered, trying his best to sound casual. No reason to give Shay any ammunition.

"You lied to me, didn't you?" Shay accused.

"Huh? What are you talking about?"

"There's something off. I can tell it by the way you're talking."

What the fuck? I don't know what she's thinking half the time, but she can figure out what's going on with me by my voice over a cell phone from halfway across the world?

James grunted. "I'm talking like I always talk. What's different about it?"

"There's something there. I can hear it. Let me guess. Are you in the middle of killing all the Mafia in Vegas off? Am I going to see a big news report about some casino getting blown up?"

"Nah. Still just trying to track down the bounty. I..." James glanced down at the glowing arrow. "Uh, I only know the general direction of the guy, so still in the tracking part of the job."

"The direction? Some sort of magic tracking like I suggested?"

"Yeah, exactly."

"Glad to see you can be reasonable every now and again, James," Shay replied. "The important thing is taking this guy down, not preserving your precious sense of simplicity."

James grunted. "Whatever. You won, and I'm using magic to track the asshole down. Then I'll keep it simple as I beat his ass."

Shay snickered. "By the way, it's not about winning or losing. It's just about…we'll call it personal growth. So, where are you now? You tracking this guy back to California or some shit like that? What's going on around you?"

The two cops watched him, their brows furrowed in concentration. They obviously were trying to reconstruct the part of the conversation they couldn't hear.

James cleared his throat. "Just… Vegas still. Dry desert. I'm actually at the edge of town, now, heading toward some mountains. Nothing special."

"Just making sure you're not driving into a trap."

"No traps. I don't think the guy I'm following is even paying that much attention to me."

Shay laughed. "Poor baby. That has to hurt the old male ego."

"I don't give a shit if he knows I'm coming. It won't stop me. It's not even important he knows who I am when I take his ass out. This is about helping the girl."

"You've got a real soft spot for helping orphaned little girls, don't you?"

"Yeah, I guess I do." It wasn't exactly news to him.

"Anyway, what you're describing doesn't sound like an area where a bunch of Mafia guys would hang out. I guess I'll let you go then. Don't want to distract you from the single guy you'll be beating up." Shay snickered. "Talk to you later."

"Sometimes it's ten guys, and sometimes it's one. Just the way the job works. Talk to you later." James hung up and set his phone down.

The cops continued eyeing him, and James realized he had no clue if there were local ordinances against talking on your phone while driving. Had they been pissed off by his flagrant disregard for their traffic laws?

No, that didn't make sense. They were bending far more important rules in this investigation than traffic laws. This was about them wanting to invade his privacy.

"Something you need to know?" James rumbled.

Detective West nodded toward the phone. "Who was that? It sounded like you were talking about the investigation with her."

"This isn't an investigation to me. It's a hunt."

"Same difference."

"I don't have the kind of rules you guys have." James shrugged. "It was my girlfriend. She just wanted to know what I was up to. She's overseas right now on a job. We like to talk to each other when we're out of town doing shit. Keeps us from getting as worried and all that crap."

"So she *was* asking about the Red Eyes Killer just now." The detective frowned.

"Not exactly. Not at first. She just wanted to know if I was about to do something dangerous and if it'd involve the Mafia."

"The Mafia?"

James nodded. "Yeah, because of my history of having loud *disagreements* with organized crime."

"Is that what you're calling wiping out the Harriken?"

The bounty hunter offered a quick shrug in reply.

The detective chuckled. "You're going to age that woman prematurely."

"Huh?"

"It sucks dating or being married to a cop, but you take rough jobs to the next level. It's got to be very hard on your girlfriend to date a man with such a dangerous job."

James chuckled. "Doubt it."

The two cops stared at him for a moment.

"Why do you say that?" Detective Lafayette inquired, breaking into the conversation. "Is she some sort of danger junkie? Is that why you two get together?"

"Nah. She's not afraid of danger, but she's not a danger junkie. Her job's pretty dangerous, too. I think she's just worried that I'm having more fun than she is." James furrowed his brow. "Huh. Maybe she's more of a danger junkie than I thought."

The detective laughed. "Your girlfriend is a nutjob, Brownstone, like you. But I mean that with respect."

James shrugged. "She has to be to like a guy like me."

"Doesn't look that big," James commented as the laboratory grew closer. It looked like a small building to him, but he wasn't an expert on biotech companies and their typical facility layouts.

"It's all inside the mountain," explained Detective West. "The front part's basically just a huge-ass reception area with elevators. Don't know how far it goes in or down."

"Oh. A weird place to build a lab. Were they afraid of getting hit by a nuke or something?"

"Who knows?"

James slowed and pulled off the road. The gate was visible in the distance, but still far away. The revelation of the true size of the lab reinforced that he needed to approach the situation with more information in hand.

"What are you doing?" Detective West asked.

James grabbed his phone. "I don't want to go in there blind. Gonna call a buddy. I sent him a text earlier to ask if he could check out this place for me once you told me about it. I'm sure he's got all sorts of useful shit for me now, especially since I'm paying him a decent chunk of money."

"Wait, we just told you about that place not all that long ago."

"Yeah, so?"

Detective West shook his head, smirking. "Even if he's the best researcher in the world, I doubt some guy you know is going to turn up a bunch of information that *we* don't know in less than an hour. Show us what you've got, Brownstone."

James shrugged and dialed Peyton. The man picked up the first ring.

"I'm gonna put you on speaker," the bounty hunter explained. "So keep it to the important shit."

"Okay," Peyton replied.

James assumed the researcher was careful enough to understand that a slip-up like mentioning his name might endanger him or even Shay. The bounty hunter activated speaker mode.

"Tell me what you've got."

"I'm emailing you the layout for the place, including the hidden blueprints for several of their secret lab levels." This time Peyton's voice was electronically distorted.

He's being more more careful than I thought he would be. Good job, Peyton.

"Got a few codes in there," the researcher continued, "but they're from this morning, so if they've changed them already, sorry. By the way, even though it's called Anders Laboratory, it's not owned by Doctor Anders. Sure, he runs it and is nominally the CEO, but he's not the one really calling the shots."

"Who is then?"

"His investors, aka the local Mafia. They're dumping a lot of money into that place through several shell companies. They've put a lot of effort into not being found easily."

The detectives both frowned.

James grunted. "So I might be making new friends if I knock too hard?"

"You're so good at making friends, Brownstone."

"It's a talent. What can I say?"

Not that he gave that much of a shit. When it came to organized crime, James figured he'd already set a good example with the Harriken. If mobster fucks didn't want him knocking on their doors, they should make sure their labs weren't letting crazed magically-modified killers who butchered people right in front of their kids into the world.

"I'm never gonna hear the end of this from... Uh, forget that. Go on."

Is this what men mean about women always being right and women's intuition?

Peyton cleared his throat, which sounded odd with the electronic distortion. "Just so you know, even though they've tried to hide it with fake manifests, there's a shit-load of materials being shipped to that place that are…shall we say, not for general use."

"What the fuck does that mean? Is it some sort of drug lab?"

"Nothing like that. It's just that they've got stuff you only use for magic going into that place, and there's way too much for it just to be incidental shit. They've got a pretty decent supplier, judging by the volume."

Detective West whistled. "Okay, I admit, you're good. We had no idea the Mafia was tied to this place. If we'd known that, we could have gotten warrants to tear this place apart."

"I am damned good. Maybe the best. At worst, second best—in the world, just to be clear."

"You should help the police out. With talents like that, we could clear a lot of cases."

"You got money? Lots of money?"

Detective West snorted. "What about helping the public? Helping criminal victims? What about the good feelings you'll get from public service?"

"Good feelings don't buy food or pay the rent. Anyway, Brownstone, the blueprints should already be in your mail. If you need anything else, give me a call." Peyton hung up.

"Cynical bastard, isn't he?" the detective muttered.

James shrugged. "Doesn't make him wrong."

Fifteen minutes later, the three men had reviewed the blueprints and understood the general layout of the facility. It wasn't all that complicated, but the presence of a several "experimental subject floors" didn't exactly relieve anyone's tension.

"What if they've got more in there?" Detective West offered. "More freaks, that is."

James shrugged. "They aren't in town, so that means they've at least got them locked up. The way I figure it, if I end up going in there guns blazing, you cops will have to follow me because of the risk to public safety. Then if you happen to find something illegal, too bad for Doctor Anders and the Mafia."

The bounty hunter's gaze dropped to the brightly glowing arrow. The Red Eyes Killer was close, and soon Dina's father would get the vengeance the girl wanted and deserved.

He pushed open his door.

A mask of confusion settled over both cop's faces.

"Where you going, Brownstone?" Detective West asked. "You're not going to jog there from all the way over there, are you? I'm sure we can at least get inside the gate with our badges."

James shook his head. "No, I just need to make a call to someone about a little angel."

R ed Eyes stood on the top of the roof aiming one of his stolen rifles. He chuckled and squeezed the trigger, spitting bullets into the distance. Glass shattered and blood splattered on the walls as bullet after bullet pelted the small guard shack near the front gate. When it clicked empty, he tossed the rifle to the side and started flinging the grenades from a looted tactical belt, laughing the whole time.

Between the security team and the bounty hunter, he'd collected a few toys. He preferred killing people with his own abilities, but it was a fun way to start. It wasn't like he could stab a man from fifty yards away in any case.

Red Eyes leapt from the roof and landed on the ground with a thud as an alarm blared over loudspeakers. He pulled around the other rifle strapped over his shoulder.

His time of hiding in the shadows was over. He *wanted* his enemies to see who was coming for them now.

"Yes, yes. Fear the chaos. Fear *me*, and know that death stalks you."

"Shit," James muttered as he stopped the F-350 at the gate. The security guard had been shredded, and his shack resembled Swiss cheese from the bullets. The crack of gunfire filled the air, and smoke rose into the sky from burning vehicles.

Detective West yanked out his phone. "I'm calling for AET."

"Fine, but it's gonna take them way too long to get here. I'm going in." James grabbed his healing potion from the back of his glovebox and the grenade he'd hidden under the seat. "You guys should stay here until the shooting and explosions die down unless you want to die early."

The detectives looked uncomfortable with the idea, but they nodded in agreement.

Sorry, Shay, guess this is going to involve more of a big show than I planned.

He could hear *both* his girls telling him not to be a dumbass in his head.

James stepped out of the truck and reached into the guard shack. The poor security guard was hamburger on the floor.

Sorry I couldn't stop this fucker sooner, pal.

The bounty hunter slapped a large blue button, hoping it was the right control, and the metal gate ground open.

He took a deep breath and tossed Detective West his keys. "Don't fuck up my truck. I love that truck almost as much as I love my girlfriend."

The detective chuckled. "I'll keep that in mind."

James rushed through the opening in the gate toward

the rifle reports now echoing from inside the building ahead.

I'm coming, Red Eyes.

Red Eyes hissed as bullet after bullet struck him. He rushed forward to impale one man with a tentacle through his throat before cleaving another almost in half at the waist with a bone blade.

He laughed and tossed the first man at a few security guards. Blood sprayed from him like a sprinkler until the body collided with the other guards.

Red Eyes was on them in a blur. He hacked away, enjoying their dying screams as he cut them apart piece by piece.

"Glorious! I will no longer hide, for I am Death. Death does not hide in the shadows at night. Death stalks you boldly no matter where you go."

The mutant spun, seeking new prey, but there was no one left alive. He'd hoped to kill the receptionist last, having enjoyed the frozen terror on her face, but now he couldn't find her.

"Run deeper into the lab, little sheep. It will just make the chase that much more delicious."

Red Eyes hissed. A few of his wounds throbbed and didn't close, so he grabbed a dead guard and opened his mouth.

"You were weak, but you'll still make me stronger." He bit into the man's neck.

"We should wait for AET," Detective Lafayette insisted. "This is way beyond us."

Detective West shook his head. "Fuck that. We need to get in there. We're out in the middle of nowhere. We don't have time to wait for reinforcements."

"And do what, exactly? Brownstone's going to do his thing."

"He's also right. We need to get in there and collect any evidence there might be about what's going on. If we wait too long, they'll destroy the records or self-destruct or some shit, for all we know. This place is responsible for a bunch of dead parents and emotionally-scarred kids. We need to make sure we have what we need to track down every fucker responsible for the Red Eyes Killer." He threw the truck into gear. "This isn't a debate. We're going."

A few minutes of jogging brought James to the parking lot in front of the white main building. Bullet-riddled and scorched bodies decorated the area, but he didn't spot any signs of mutilation. An enemy who used a gun was an enemy James knew how to handle.

Not so special in the end, asshole?

Two security guards in blue uniforms popped from behind a large cargo truck and lifted their rifles. Their eyes screamed fear.

"Who the fuck are you?" one of them barked.

"Look at his fucking face." The other sneered. "He's a freak. XJ422 must have already freed some of the other samples. Take him out."

James ducked as bullets whizzed over his head. The slap of boots on asphalt alerted him to their positions. The trigger-happy guards were trying to flank him. He waited until they closed, then leapt up to deliver an uppercut to the closest man. He flew back and landed with a crash on the hood of a nearby Jaguar. The car alarm blared.

"What the fuck?" the other man growled.

The bounty hunter sent a throwing knife into his shooting arm before the man had recovered from his surprise, then head-butted him before the guard had stopped yelping.

The security guard slumped to the ground, unconscious but still alive.

James retrieved his knife. "Sorry, assholes. Can't let you kill me, but I'm cutting you a break since you thought I was a friend of Red Eyes."

He turned to leave but spun back to the downed guards with a smile. If he were back in LA he would have gone to his warehouse first and shown up at the lab armed to the teeth, but he wasn't supposed to even be in Vegas for bounty hunting, let alone for a level-four magical mutant. He'd come to eat some of God's own barbeque before heading home.

A single spare magazine for his .45 and some knives wouldn't be enough. He grabbed a rifle and retrieved their spare magazines from their belt pouches.

James grunted. Heckler & Koch wasn't his favorite

brand and assault rifles weren't his favorite weapon, but with all the dead security guards lying around, at least he'd have plenty of ammo.

The bounty hunter bounded toward the door. The sound of gunfire had become sporadic, then absent as he closed on the main building. Red Eyes must have been winning, especially since the main alarm was still blaring.

I don't care if they take you out or I take you out, as long as you don't leave this place alive, asshole.

Shards of glass marked the remains of the front door. James readied his rifle and ran toward the entrance, searching for targets. Bodies covered a white floor painted with a fresh coat of red blood.

A few bodies near the front had shrapnel or bullet wounds, but as James moved farther in, limbs and heads were separated from their bodies.

"Definitely Red Eyes," James mumbled. A survey of the area revealed two elevator doors. Bodies and body parts were piled up in front of one, and the door was marked with bloody handprints.

According to Peyton's information, James could take the elevator to the next floor without a code. The floor contained nothing of importance, just the cafeteria and a few other amenities like a small gym, but if Red Eyes didn't have any other access codes, that was where he'd be.

The bounty hunter took a deep breath. Killing the bounty meant he'd likely get no money. Most cities claimed you could still recover a portion. Las Vegas had stated he could get half, but in practice, once you got through all the appeals and paperwork, killing a bounty without dead-or-alive status meant a bounty hunter earned zilch.

James didn't care. Red Eyes wasn't some misguided cartel thug. He was a vicious, remorseless killer who snuffed out lives for simple enjoyment. Even King Pyro had practiced more restraint.

I'm putting your ass in the ground so Dina can get some sort of closure, unlike what I got. A worry-free life is worth a little bounty money. Fuck, it's worth a lot *of bounty money.*

James had just turned toward the door when the elevator dinged.

He raised his HK, his eyes narrowed.

A glowing-red-eyed bloody mess walked out of the elevator with a smile on his face. Red Eyes raised both his arms, both currently tipped in crimson-stained bone blades.

"It was easier to kill down there. Fewer guns." Red Eyes let out a throaty chuckle. "I have to give you credit. Your security is better than when I escaped." His smile vanished. "It's frustrating, not being able to get to the others. Give me your codes, little security man, or die."

James snorted. "Do I fucking *look* like I work here, asshole?"

The arrogance faded from Red Eyes' face. "Who are you?"

"James Brownstone." The bounty hunter waited for that revelation to sink in.

Joy lit the mutant's face. "I don't remember much. My mind...the process took it, but I know you. Class-six bounty hunter. Wonderful. *Perfect.*"

"Glad you know the level of ass-kicking that's coming your way. I've got one question for you before I send you to hell, asshole."

"Your arrogance is appreciated. Assimilating you will make me more powerful."

James grimaced. "You're talking about eating me, aren't you?"

"You will become one with something stronger."

"If that's what all this shit is about, then why kill parents? Why fuck up little kids?"

"Killing parents was just for fun." Red Eyes inhaled deeply. "Killing bounty hunters, though, will improve my strength and skills. Once I kill you, my name will be a word of terror that echoes across the country."

James snorted. "Talk about your delusions of grandeur."

"Delusions of grandeur? No, James Brownstone. They call this place a lab, but they took the flesh of the weak and sculpted it with science and the help of dark magic. It's a temple for birthing new gods."

The bounty hunter sighed and shook his head. "Asshole, you're not even a level five. I'd maybe let you have the 'I'm a god' speech if you were level five."

Red Eyes' face contorted in rage. "Once I kill you, I'll prove that I *am* level five. Fine, James Brownstone, be a sacrifice to the new god of Death and Chaos!"

"Fuck you. This is for Dina and all the other kids." James fired a burst into Red Eyes.

The mutant jerked back but grinned. "How many times do you think I've been shot?"

James shrugged. "Sometimes it's just a matter of trying

until you win." He flipped the rifle to automatic and held down the trigger.

The mutant kept jerking and hissing, but he didn't go down. The bounty hunter yanked up his frag grenade and tossed it with his free hand before his gun clicked empty.

The grenade exploded right in front of the mutant, and when Red Eyes stood, blood oozed from all over his body. A rough shrapnel outline of his body marred the elevator door.

James snickered. "It's like some shit from the old cartoons I used to watch."

Red Eyes growled. "How dare you mock me? I will torture you slowly before I finish you off and assimilate your DNA."

"That shit sounds complicated. Most people just threaten to kill me. Whatever." James threw the rifle at the mutant and charged him.

Red Eyes batted the rifle away, but James had already closed the distance. The bounty hunter's shoulder smashed into the mutant's chest and slammed him into the elevator doors, leaving a body-sized dent around the mutant's outline

James pounded the asshole's face with several quick jabs. Having the amulet would have upped his defenses, but he was strong 24/7 and without any weird alien thought-whispers.

Red Eyes' head snapped back with each blow. James wasn't holding back. If the mutant had been a normal man, his face would have already been caved in.

Wonder if everyone on my home planet is as strong as I am, or if this is some sort of shit where I grew up in a different place so I'm tougher.

The mutant slashed James' shoulder and the bounty hunter jumped back with a grunt, the wound throbbing. Another slash sliced into James' thigh, but he gritted his teeth and ignored the pain.

Guess it's a good thing I brought the healing potion.

Red Eyes staggered forward, his leathery and mottled face even more misshapen after James' beating.

"You…are…nothing, James Brownstone. You…will…not…defeat…me."

The bounty hunter shook his head. "Didn't know it hurt so much to get your ass beat by nothing."

James flung several knives in rapid succession at the mutant's shoulders and ducked a bone blade as he rushed toward the wounded mutant again. The mutant's other arm contorted and twisted as James slammed an elbow into Red Eyes' throat, then grabbed the mutant's changing arm to snap it over his knee. The crunch echoed in the vast reception area.

Red Eyes howled, and his arm twitched and thrashed. Barbs sprouted from it, some ripping into James' clothing and flesh.

The bounty hunter launched another series of punches into the wounded mutant's body and head and the killer staggered back, the red of his eyes now blood and not his natural glow.

James yanked out his K-Bar and jammed it into the mutant's heart three or four times before adding a few new holes to his head.

Gotta keep this shit balanced.

The room started to darken, its shadows growing. Red Eyes collapsed to his knees and crawled back.

"No, you don't, asshole," James growled. "I'm not fucking done with you." He sheathed his knife and walked behind the twitching and thrashing mutant. He yanked him up and snapped his neck. "That's for Dina's dad."

The mutant didn't slump, just kept thrashing. James tossed him to the ground and pinned Red Eyes with his knee.

James raised his knife again. "Wish I'd packed a machete. It really makes this shit easier." Five quick slashes later, only a few strands of muscle connected Red Eyes' head to his body. "And this is for everyone else you killed, you piece of shit."

The bounty hunter grunted and jerked the head away from the body. The corpse slumped to the ground. James tossed the head next to it and stood.

Heavy breaths followed as the numbness of adrenaline gave way to sharp pain. Deep wounds in his shoulder and thigh continued to seep blood, and in addition, a dozen minor lacerations covered his body.

James opened the healing potion and downed it in one gulp. Thirty seconds later, he was a new man in need of a new outfit.

Something scratched the ground behind him. His hand dropped to his .45, and he spun toward the noise.

Detectives West and Lafayette held up their hands.

"I told you to stay in the fucking truck." James holstered his gun.

The detectives slowly lowered his arms.

Detective West grinned. "Don't worry, didn't even

scratch the paint." He looked around and shook his head. "We got here in time to overhear some of that asshole's rant. Between that and the bodies, it's more than enough to crack this place open with a search warrant."

"Good," James growled. "The kids of Las Vegas should never have to deal with this kind of shit again."

24

Trey, Charlyce, and James stood in the playroom at the CPS building, waiting for a staffer to bring in the girl. The door opened, and Dina rushed in with a smile. She hugged Charlyce and then James.

"Guess I'm chopped liver," Trey mumbled.

The girl hugged him too, and all the adults laughed.

Dina's smile disappeared, and she stared at James with mournful eyes. "Red Eyes is gone?"

James nodded. "I made sure he'll never hurt anyone again."

The girl started crying. "I want my daddy. Where do I go now?"

Charlyce smiled. "I would have loved to have taken you, but they don't let people like me foster kids. It'll be a while before the system trusts me."

James smiled down at the girl. "Don't worry, I've already made some calls. I've got a better idea."

James didn't think anything of a huge road trip, but he was surprised the girl didn't have any problems as they drove straight back from Las Vegas to Los Angeles. It must have helped that the little angel slept most of the way.

As he turned onto a side street leading to their destination, he chuckled.

Charlyce looked at him from the passenger seat of his truck. She'd insisted on riding with Dina the whole way. Trey had been disappointed, but he'd had to drive his truck back anyway.

"What's so funny, Mr. Brownstone?"

"This place isn't any safer than Vegas. I've dealt with more strange criminals with powers here than anywhere, but it still feels good to be home. I feel safer here. More relaxed. Everything seems simpler, somehow. Guess that's what 'home' means."

"Home," Charlyce echoed. She sighed. "That's still a hard idea to wrap my head around."

"Trey's a good man. He'll give you all the help you need."

"I only hope I'm worthy of that help."

"Don't hope. Just be." James pulled into the driveway of a modest but large two-story house with a new coat of brown paint. He was glad to see his money being well spent on helping the orphans.

The front door opened, and Father McCartney stepped outside.

James and Charlyce stepped out of the truck, and the woman picked up the sleeping Dina. The girl stirred in her arms and yawned.

The little angel's eyes fluttered. "Where are we?"

"This is the place I told you about," James explained. "It's an orphanage. I visit it from time to time."

"You do?"

He nodded. "Yeah. I grew up here myself, and it's one of the reasons I'm the man I am today."

Father McCartney smiled at the comment.

Dina rested her head against Charlyce's shoulder. "Do you protect the kids in the orphanage?"

James nodded. "Yeah, I do. Angels aren't just nice messengers, after all. They are warriors too. Here, the angels protect the children."

Father McCartney cleared his throat. "Welcome, Dina. I'm glad to have you with us."

An older girl stepped outside and waved from the porch.

The priest leaned forward to pat Dina on the head. "Would you like to see your new room?"

"Yes, please."

Charlyce set the girl on the ground. "I'll visit you next weekend, my little angel."

Dina gave the woman another tight hug before scampering off to the house.

Father McCartney shook his head and turned to James. "The hand of God has guided this, James."

The bounty hunter shrugged. "Doesn't it guide everything?"

"No, I'm just saying that even with the stock money we only have so many resources, but the anonymous benefactor upped their payments recently. We wouldn't have been able to take the girl otherwise. I think we'll need to hire someone, or maybe reach out for more volunteers, though. Things are stretched, even with the help of the older kids."

Charlyce smiled at the priest. "I'll volunteer." She laughed. "Assuming you don't have a problem with me being Methodist."

The priest chuckled. "No, I value any and all help."

The woman looked at the orphanage. "God gave me another chance, so I want to make the best of it. Plus, I owe that girl."

James watched in silence, pleased with himself and not wanting to ruin the moment with some blunt comment.

See, Shay? I'm learning.

Father McCartney looked confused. "Owe her? How could you owe Dina?"

"I'm back in the world and with my family because of what she lost. The least I can do is be there for her."

"That's all any of us can ever do," James rumbled.

Lieutenant Hall secured her helmet and lifted the railgun, then initiated the charge cycle and stepped out of the back of the van.

Unlike last time, she wouldn't wait until half the team was on the ground to fire the weapon. Using a weapon that was so unreliable wasn't on her list of favorite things, but Tessa Vansant did top the current list of Maria's least favorite things.

"Everyone's in position, Lieutenant," Weber called over his radio. "I'm glad the country club agreed to this plan."

"Yeah, no innocent people will be getting hurt today."

The media was still publicly reporting that the Nadina event was on, but the country club and event organizers had reached out to all ticket holders to let them know it'd be rescheduled and not to discuss it. Miraculously no one had. They'd also been able to verify that Tessa Vansant wasn't one of the ticket holders.

So now it was just a simple matter of waiting for the level-five bounty to show up.

This isn't like last time. This bitch goes down fast.

"We got eyes on a car, Lieutenant," Weber informed her.

Maria set up the bipod for the railgun and laid the weapon on the ground. She aimed it and waited as a rusty old Chrysler sedan pulled into the parking lot filled with luxury vehicles.

Not even trying to blend in, huh, Tessa?

Several AET officers popped up from behind cars. Rocket drones rose from behind shrubs, their deadly payloads ready.

Maria tapped a mic control on her wrist. "Tessa Vansant. This is LAPD AET. You are to immediately come out with your hands up and surrender. You're under arrest for homicide and terrorism. Any sudden movements will be considered hostile actions, and you will be fired upon." She switched back to radio transmit mode.

Good. Now the formalities are over. We've got you, bitch.

"She's doing something, Lieutenant!"

Maria upped the magnification of her suit goggles. Tessa was chanting and waving her wand.

"Light her up!" the lieutenant barked. She squeezed the railgun's trigger and the weapon hummed, then died. "Son of a bitch." She hopped up and kicked it.

A swarm of bullets and rockets slammed into Tessa's car. Maria averted her gaze as the sedan blasted into the air, engulfed by a fireball.

She blinked as she spotted a couple of news helicopters hovering in the sky.

Shit. They were expecting Nadina, but they're seeing all this.

Maria grabbed her sidearm and sent, "Advance and confirm kill."

The AET team marched toward the burning wreck, their weapons at the ready.

A fiery form pushed open the door, and the flames parted to reveal the witch. Tessa rolled out of the car, her face locked in rage. A glowing shield of emerald light surrounded her body, and three glyphs of light winked into existence above her.

"Take cover and open fire!" Maria ordered.

The harsh crack of rifles filled the air, and bullets poured into Tessa. Her shield flashed brightly with each hit.

The three glyphs above her formed into the same demons they'd seen on drone feeds from the farmers' market incident. According to records, Tessa claimed they were an ancient Sumerian demon called a Rabisu. Maria didn't care what they were called, only that they were stopped.

The Rabisu launched energy blasts toward the police. One man took a direct hit and flew through the air, screaming. His new deflector darkened but didn't turn black. He rolled on the ground, moaning.

Maria unloaded her pistol at Tessa, ignoring the Rabisu,

but they didn't ignore her. An energy blast smashed into the car next to her.

The resulting explosion launched the lieutenant into a nearby windshield and pain zapped through her body. An anti-magic deflector could absorb magic, but it didn't do much to protect her against regular blasts. Her armor had helped, but she would be feeling that hit for a few weeks.

The lieutenant extricated herself from the windshield and dropped to the ground. She grabbed an incendiary grenade and arced it toward one of the Rabisu with a call of "incendiary out."

The beast roared as the flames scorched its scales.

"You like that, you son of a bitch?"

Another wave of rocket drones closed on the parking lot and released their payloads into the Rabisu. One collapsed to the ground, dissolving into a puddle of green ichor, and the bullets and stun blasts striking the second had it on its knees. It started dissolving a few seconds later.

Maria sprinted toward the nearest AET van and leapt into it, an energy blast from the last Rabisu missing her by inches. Some poor jerk's Audi took the hit instead and the vehicle melted into slag.

The lieutenant grabbed a rifle. Since the fight had begun Tessa hadn't done much but crouch behind a car, her annoying energy shield protecting her. Maria had worried about the witch raining down spells or summoning more beasts, but she must have already been at her limit.

We can fucking win this.

Maria slapped a magazine into the rifle and readied the weapon, then hopped back out of the van and fired a burst at the remaining Rabisu before darting between cars. Another vehicle exploded behind her, but she continued charging forward until she had Tessa in her sights. She aimed at the woman's head and fired.

The bullets bounced off the shield, and the woman glared at Maria. Sweat coated Tessa's face and neck.

"Having trouble, bitch?" Maria called. She dropped a hand to a sonic grenade. "Sonic out!"

The grenade slammed into the shield. The windows of several nearby cars shattered, and even with her helmet on and the distance between them Maria's ears rang.

Tessa screamed and dropped her wand, and her shield vanished.

Doesn't stop sound, huh?

Maria whipped up her rifle and put a three-round burst into the witch's center of mass.

She screamed and fell back, blood pooling beneath her. The remaining Rabisu dissolved instantly.

The AET lieutenant rushed toward the witch.

Tessa lay on the ground, coughing up blood.

Maria sneered, but the witch couldn't see it through her helmet. "You should have just surrendered, you psycho bitch."

"It's fine," Tessa whispered. "It turns out *you're* alive, and *I'm* just a ghost." She let out a strangled laugh before her head slumped to the side and her chest stopped moving.

"Suspect terminated." Maria turned to survey the area. A couple of men had their helmets off and were standing with the aid of others, but she didn't see anyone lying on the ground with a hole in their chest.

"Minor injuries for several people, Lieutenant."

Sergeant Weber stepped toward her. "Lost two deflectors. Two guys have bad burns, but that's about it."

Maria pulled off her helmet and looked from burning wreck to burning wreck. Dozens of cars were now smoldering ruins. "Fuck. We won, but we let half this fucking parking lot go up. We're as bad as Brownstone." She slapped her helmet against her forehead. "We fucking *suck*."

25

Trey's foot kept twitching as he sat on his grandmother's couch with his Aunt Charlyce. They'd been waiting for Nana to get back from the store, so he still didn't know how things would go down. He'd texted his grandmother before leaving Las Vegas, but her response had been very blunt and to the point.

She wanted to meet her estranged daughter, but she was making no promises past that, and she didn't want to talk with her on the phone, but face-to-face.

His grandmother wasn't to be fucked with. The old woman had lived decades in a slowly dying neighborhood, surrounded by gangbangers and other criminals. She didn't take shit from anyone, and that included her family.

What the fuck do I do if this goes down the toilet? I want to have my family together, but I can't piss off Nana.

Trey ran a hand through his hair. Bile rose in his throat. He hadn't been this nervous since a level-two bounty ambushed him in an alley and got off three shots before he knew what was happening.

Charlyce was an aunt to him, but a daughter to his grandmother—a daughter who'd betrayed her trust and thrown her life away on drugs and alcohol. She'd admitted her mistakes, and Trey of all people wasn't one to throw stones about past sins, but his grandmother had lived a clean life during which she was loyal to her family. She'd even maintained her relationship with him when he'd run with the gangs.

She needed to accept that the past was the past like he had. It was rare that anyone got a second chance. It was even rarer that an entire family got a second chance, or three generations of one, for that matter.

Please, Nana. We've lost so much. Just let our family come back together. Accept her for who she is now and don't push her away for who she was.

Lights pierced the darkness in the driveway, giving way to an Uber carrying the old woman. She stepped out of the car, her paper bag in hand, and made her way to the door with a frown on her wrinkled face.

Trey hurried to open the door and take the bag from her. As she handed the bag to him as she kept her gaze locked on her wayward daughter, studying her with the heavy weight of seven years' disappointment in her eyes.

Trey carried the bag to the kitchen but kept watching the two. A tense silence smothered the room as Trey's aunt and Nana stared at each other, and his heart galloped.

Shit. It's not gonna happen.

A single tear slid down the older woman's face and all the suspicion and anger disappeared, replaced by bittersweet joy. Trey's heart soared.

His grandmother wiped the tear away. "Seven years,

sweetie. I always hoped and prayed that you'd come back to me someday. I don't blame you for anything. We've all made our mistakes. I could have been a better mother, but it doesn't matter." She held out her arms. "It doesn't matter now because my prayers have been answered."

Aunt Charlyce ran into her mother's arms and both women starting sobbing.

Trey set the bag down and looked away, his own eyes watering. He pulled out a handkerchief and wiped them. A slob used their sleeve; a smooth and refined man used a handkerchief. That was what the websites said, anyway.

"We're a family again," his grandmother managed to get out between sobs. "And I'm the luckiest woman alive. I didn't think I'd live to see this day."

"We're all lucky, Nana," Trey offered. "Luckiest damned family on the planet."

It took a good fifteen minutes for everyone to calm down and put the groceries away before they all returned to sit in the living room.

Trey's grandmother dabbed her eyes, the tears of joy still threatening to return. "Where you planning on living, Charlyce?"

"I…don't know. Trey said I could stay with him."

Trey nodded. "Sure thing."

His grandmother frowned. "Hush now, boy. She's *my* daughter, not yours. I have plenty of room."

Aunt Charlyce smiled. "Thanks, Mama."

Trey shrugged. "Not gonna complain. A grown man needs to have his space."

"I'm gonna be working, too."

Her mother's eyes widened. "You've already got a job lined up?"

"I talked to Mr. Brownstone about giving her a job." Trey smiled and adjusted his tie. "We need an administrative assistant at the Brownstone Agency, and if you can't trust family, who can you trust?"

His grandmother smiled, her face awash in pride like he hadn't seen since... Hell, *ever*. "Look at you now, Trey! You used to be a no-good hoodlum bum."

"Hey now, Nana. Let's watch it. I wasn't *that* bad."

She shook her head. "We both know it, boy. You running the neighborhood with that gang causing trouble, fighting with people? You know how I'd sometimes cry, thinking, 'What have I done to deserve this?' That boy's gonna end up in prison and break my heart."

Trey groaned, and his aunt laughed.

"But things are different now. You've got a proper job helping people."

"I'm still fighting," he grumbled.

"Only bad people now. I get that. Sometimes you just have to hit a man with your cane."

"I was only fighting bad people before." Trey smirked. "And I'm not old. *I* don't hit people with canes, *you* do."

"Keep it up, boy, and I'll hit *you* with my cane." His grandmother glowered, then her expression softened. "The point is, Trey, I'm proud of you. You helped save my daughter, and you're giving back to this community instead of taking. It don't matter that you used to be a hoodlum. No man can change the past, not even those magic folks from Oriceran, but every man can change his future."

Trey rolled his eyes. "I wasn't a hoodlum." He motioned to his suit. "Does a hoodlum wear suits like this?"

His grandmother laughed. "You weren't wearing those suits before, boy."

A couple of hours of reminiscing later, Trey hugged his aunt and grandmother before heading outside to his F-350. Now that the Las Vegas adventure was over, he needed to concentrate on local bounty hunting and helping improve things within the growing Brownstone Agency. Even though Royce was still whipping the men into shape, Trey would soon need to guide the first few who were ready to graduate to something other than talking to people for information.

The Brownstone Agency would become an army of bounty hunters, sweeping across Los Angeles until there was no one with a bounty left to arrest. Sure, they might not be able to handle killers like King Pyro or Red Eyes, but those kinds of threats were rare.

Maybe someday we'll set up teams in different cities. San Francisco branch. San Diego branch. Even some poor suckers in Sacramento. Tokyo branch. Now that shit would be sweet.

He toyed with the thought as he drove to his place. The problem with most bounty hunters was that they were just in the game for the money. From what he'd read on the net there were other bounty-hunting firms, but none of any decent size—and none that had a man like James Brownstone at their head.

Reputation was a big thing, and James had earned his rep the hard way—through buckets of blood and piles of bullets.

Even if more people started firms to compete with the Brownstone Agency, the city would ultimately win. It'd mean fewer criminals poking their heads up.

Trey chuckled. He'd been a criminal not all that long ago, but he already was thinking of himself as the hand of the law and about how he could help run criminals off.

Not like this city wouldn't be better off with fuckers like the Demon Generals gone. Too bad most of those bitches don't have bounties.

He parked his truck at the curb. He needed to get a place with a nice driveway, or even a garage. He'd gone through the trouble to get a sweet-ass truck like his mentor, so he needed to treat it with as much love as James did his.

Trey had just stepped out of his truck when a pair of highlights shined around the corner. His hand slipped inside his jacket to his holster. While he didn't know of any immediate threats to his life, he hadn't forgotten how James'd had to beat down some Demon Generals who had rolled into the neighborhood to extract revenge on Trey. Just because he'd left the gang lifestyle didn't mean he'd escaped his gang past.

Even though that shit had been about helping James and not the gang.

The source of the highlights slowed, and Trey dropped

his hand when he recognized the other F-350 that drove around the neighborhood.

James pulled his truck to a stop and rolled down his window. "Hey, Trey."

"Damn, big man," Trey called. "You made me nervous, and I was *this close* to capping your ass. I'd never live that shit down. They'd run me not only out of the neighborhood but out of the state."

"If you could take me out, half the city would build a statue to you to celebrate how badass you are." James gave a light chuckle. "And it'd be pretty fucking embarrassing if I ended up surviving all the shit I have just to get killed by one of my employees by accident."

"You're telling me." Trey whistled. "How about that Vegas shit? I don't think either of us knew what we were getting into."

James grunted. "I just wanted some barbeque. But it was a nice change of pace. I was hunting a guy instead of having a bunch of assholes hunting me. Didn't have to worry about my truck or having to blow up any buildings. It was kinda like how things used to be…simple. Or simp*ler*." He shrugged.

Trey shrugged. "Pretty sure people get that you don't fuck with James Brownstone and live by now."

"You'd think, but a lot of people are dumbasses." James looked thoughtful. "Everything go all right with your aunt?"

"Yeah. Nana was damned happy." Trey smiled. "It feels good to have my auntie back, and not only that, I'm in a position to help her. If I was still gangbanging on the streets, I wouldn't have been able to get her a job. I guess that's paying it forward. You helped me, I helped her."

"This time it's family, next time you won't know who it's for. I'm doing the same thing when I think about it."

"Paying it forward?"

James nodded. "Yeah. The priests helped me when I was an orphan. I could have ended up on the street, but because they gave a shit, I didn't end up some messed-up high-level bounty wanted for murdering people."

"That's deep, James. I'm hoping we can do the same for the rest of the boys."

"You worried?"

Trey shook his head. "Not really, but maybe there's something we can do as a company to help with that. You know, build morale and shit. I've been reading a lot about it. Leadership, organization, management, and all that shit."

James furrowed his brow. "Huh. Really? What'd you have in mind? I don't do sports. People get hurt when I try."

"I bet." Trey snapped his fingers. "How about a barbeque team? You've done competitions, and you can lead us to victory. Builds teamwork and shit, but we can also start out winners. Everyone likes being a winner."

James laughed, but stopped when Trey didn't join him.

"You're serious?" the older bounty hunter asked.

Trey snorted. "Damned right, I'm serious."

"I don't know…" James sighed. "I don't have the books I used to."

"Don't give me no shit about how you lost your signed recipe books, man. Just get some new ones." Trey pointed at James' head. "And give me a fucking break. I know you don't forget shit. How many times did you read those books? If you ever quit bounty hunting, you'd be the ultimate pitmaster. You've got a fucking encyclopedia of barbeque in that head. I say we do shit the world ain't ever seen." He slammed a fist into his palm. "And I mean shit that makes Nadina look like she's from Wyoming."

James rubbed the back of his neck and gave Trey a wide grin. "Why the hell not?"

James frowned as he approached his house. The lights in his living room were on.

Someone's really trying to piss me off.

He relaxed once the garage door opened to reveal a red Fiat Spider in the driveway.

"Guess that explains why my security system is off, but why didn't she bother to tell me she was coming home?"

James pulled into his garage and killed the engine, then stepped inside the house and around the corner. A single sock lay on the ground.

"Come on, Shay, you don't have to leave your socks all over."

He leaned over to grab the sock. Another sock lay a few feet away. He grunted and walked over to pick it up. The trail continued toward his bedroom with pants, then a shirt, bra, and panties right in front of the bed.

Shay threw back the covers to reveal her naked body and winked. "I think I need me some Stone."

James killed the lights and grinned. "Oh. In that case, I don't give a shit about a few socks on the floor."

The warmth of the sun's rays tickled Shay's face, and she awoke with a yawn. James remained asleep, snoring loudly on the opposite side of the bed. She reached over to her nightstand to check her phone. She'd sent Alison a text last night before going to sleep, but the girl, likely already asleep in Virginia, hadn't returned it.

He's ok. He had backup.

The girl's response had come in an hour before Shay had awoken.

TY, Aunt Shay. Or should I say Mom? ;-)

Shay smirked. "That girl is too damned smart."

She put the phone down and slid an arm across the chest of her sleeping man. "Next job is coming up soon. Better make sure I'm too sore to even want something by then."

Shay grinned. It'd be a fun, if exhausting, few days.

FINIS

Thank you for pulverizing the pages and making your way through the SIXTH Brownstone book, to read these *Author Notes* at the end.

When I wrote the book beats which would become *When Angels Cry*, the question I centered around was 'what kind of asshole would kill parents, and then be happy that their children were upset?'

I didn't want a person who was evil already. Rather, I wanted something to happen to the bad guy that *changed* him or her. I thought 'what would those in society be doing with this new magic? Both light magic, and dark?'

In my imagination, *EVERYONE* from the lowest hood on the street with grandiose aspirations to corporations to the dark underbelly of society on up to governments would be playing around with something they shouldn't.

Including the Mob.

In Vegas (where I perch from time to time), there is a history of the Mob. For the most part, you don't hear about it anymore, since legitimate businesses (MGM, Caesars

Entertainment, etc.) take all the press outside Vegas. I don't read much about the dark underbelly of what Vegas is like right now.

It doesn't *feel* like a Mob town. But then, a mobster would probably have to roll up in their limousine as I'm walking down the street and point to themselves and say 'Hey! I'm a mobster!' to get me to notice.

The problem with that situation is, I would have a KAJILLION questions about what's going on! I'm sure too many of those questions would get me singing with the fishes...Which might be a bit hard in a desert town.

But there is a reservoir close enough.

So no. If any mobsters are reading this right now, I really *DON'T* wish to talk with you, because my natural inquisitive self couldn't keep his fucking mouth shut.

And we wouldn't get any more Brownstone. Or Katie, or Bethany Anne... You get the picture.

As I'm typing this, I'm eating at the Pacifica Resort in Cabo San Lucas. THIS is the resort where I wrote Book 03 of The Kurtherian Gambit and coined the term (in my mind) 20 books to 50k. I'm trying to take a bit of a breather. A rest and a little relaxation.

As much as I can.

As we gear up for a monster rest of this year, and then a GODZILLA year in 2019, all of us need to sit back and take a few breaths from time to time. You, me, them... It doesn't matter.

Just breathe and relax. Enjoy the moment to the best of our abilities, and consider the awesomeness we have as authors and readers. We are enjoying THIS moment in history, when we can publish a book on Friday morning in

Naples Florida (or wherever the hell Zen Master Walking ™ is located) and you can be reading it in Germany, Canada, Japan, Australia, or even Las Vegas, Nevada just minutes (or sometimes a few hours) later.

We are all blessed by digital book distribution, and I'm so damned happy that you are enjoying it with me and the rest of us at LMBPN Publishing.

Thank you!

Ad Aeternitatem,

Michael Anderle

The Soul Stone Mage Series

* Sarah Noffke and Martha Carr *

House of Enchanted (1) - The Dark Forest (2) - Mountain of Truth (3) - Land of Terran (4) - New Egypt (5) - Lancothy (6) - Virgo (7)

The Kacy Chronicles

* A.L. Knorr and Martha Carr *

Descendant (1) - Ascendant (2) - Combatant (3) - Transcendent (4)

The Midwest Magic Chronicles

* Flint Maxwell and Martha Carr*

The Midwest Witch (1) - The Midwest Wanderer (2) - The Midwest Whisperer (3) - The Midwest War (4)

The Fairhaven Chronicles

* with S.M. Boyce *

Glow (1) - Shimmer (2) - Ember (3) - Nightfall (4)